Other works by Bruce Chester

The Eleusian Effect

The King's Betrothed

Great Short Stories, Vol. 1

The Defender
By Bruce Chester

Published by Bruce Chester
June 2020

First Printing: 2020

ISBN 978-1-71681-040-4

Published by Bruce Chester
30 Pine St. STE. 310
Gardner, MA 01440
www.brucechester.com

Ordering Information:

Special discounts are available on quantity purchases by corporations, associations, educators, and others. For details, contact the publisher at the above listed address.

U.S. trade bookstores and wholesalers: Please contact Bruce Chester Tel: (978) 514;5500 or email thebenaycompanies@gmail.com

Dedication

To My wife Ann, daughter Courtney, my siblings and my friends. I love you all very much

Thank you.

In Memoriam

My parents were always supportive of my creative activities. They enjoyed my shows, my musical performances and speeches. They didn't attend everything I did (that's probably a good thing) but they were some of my greatest fans. I miss them terribly, as my father had passed away before my first book was published. My mother suffered from dementia for the last decade before she passed away in 2019. They were amazing people and I am planning to write their story in the very near future. I dedicated a short story to my Dad that you can enjoy in Great Short Stories, Vol. I. I could go on an on.

Suffice to say that I would not be the man I am today without their love, support and guidance throughout my life. I miss them and they were taken too soon. I didn't think a Dedication was adequate to honor them, so this memorial is to remind myself how lucky I am to have had the parents I had. God Bless you, Mom and Dad.

A Word Before

Being a writer has given me a great sense of satisfaction as I love to tell stories that entertain, thrill and excite the reader. I am sensitive, however, to people's personal beliefs and feeling towards certain things, particular the famous three: politics, sex and religion. I have my own personal beliefs and as most writers will tell you, much of that shows through our work. I have always tried to use these topics sparingly in my storytelling, if at all. I avoid sexual topics as well as political for the most part, however in this particular story, I do use elements of the Catholic church as part of the framework of this story. A great amount the details are taken from past cases and modified to fit this story. Let me be clear: this is not a criticism or denigration of the Catholic faith or of any parish, archdiocese or member of the Catholic clergy. All the characters in this work are fictional, though some things, places and people are used only as template for the characters. I hope you enjoy it.

Bruce Chester

PART I: To Teach and Protect

It was a regular Friday at Langston High School. The eighth graders' hormones were raging as they do; the boys can't stop goofing around in class, the girls are giggling and gossiping about boys and make up. Not much else happens in the quiet town of Langston, Massachusetts, a sleepy old New England town about an hour west of Boston. Jack Chase, the vice principal was stern but fair. His morning routine started with him standing outside to welcome the buses and contemplate the day ahead. He loved his job and he loved his students, even when they had weekend-itis. He had been teaching for ten years after spending a successful stint in the Army. Twenty years was enough of that since his daughter was approaching high school age. He figured being a teacher would be a great way to watch his little girl grow up. He never figured he'd grow to love his new profession. Now, with his little girl in college, and his wife passed away, he would focus on other people's' kids. The public-school system was political but nothing he hadn't dealt with in the service.

"Good Morning, Mr. Chase!" The kids would blast past him through the front door. Langston Junior-Senior High School had seen better days and now that a new $80 million school was being built, the future seemed bright. Still, it was his school, having graduated 30 years ago himself. He would always have those memories, the theatrical plays, the time he almost broke his ankle playing football, that terrible piece of furniture he made in wood shop; they always made him smile. Once the buses pulled away, he went back into the school. He would teach a class every so often. He enjoyed his job but missed seeing those "A-Ha" moments from the students. He had considered stepping down and being just a teacher again, but the timing wasn't right. There were some problem students he wanted to fix before he vacated that position. He strolled into the office and checked in with the School Receptionist.

"Morning Alma."

"Morning, Mr. Chase." They were on a first name basis but never in front of the students. There were three waiting there. "What's the issue?"

"These three have early dismissal. They have notes."

"They do, do they?" he said with mock sternness. "What's the issue boys?

The oldest spoke up. "We have a funeral to go, sir. We have a note."

"So, I've heard. Lemme see." The oldest handed him a typed letter. These three were the Hanney Brothers, all about a year apart in age. The letter covered all three. "Alma, did you call their mother to confirm?"

"Not yet. She wanted to tell you directly. She asked that you call personally."

"Ok. You three get to class and I will talk to your mother."

"Thank you, Mr. Chase."

"No Problem, Guys." The boys scurried out of the office.

He turned to Alma and asked, "What time do they need to leave?"

"About 11."

"Okay." He strolled into his office and sat down. He picked up the phone and was about to dial when he noticed an odd envelope on his desk. He'd ask Alma about it later. He punched in the number and waited. The Hanney brothers were decent kids. They just had some hard luck. The official story was that about 3 years ago, their father was working as a local plant manager and died in an accident. Rumors around town said it wasn't an accident and blamed some sketchy union guys. Why they allegedly killed him was still vague. Those boys had been through enough tragedy-another funeral was the last thing they needed.

"Mrs. Hanney? Jack Chase here, Langston High. I see here the boys have a funeral to attend."

"Yes, their paternal grandmother died."

"I'm so sorry, you have my sincerest condolences."

"Thank you. I will need to pick them at 11."

"That's no problem. We'll have them ready."

"Thank you." She hung up quickly, almost as if she was being pulled away. Chase found it odd but gave it little thought. He went over to Alma, remembered the odd envelope and grabbed it. "Alma, what's this?"

"It was taped to the front door this morning. It just had your name on it."

"Weird," he thought. "Anything on the camera?"

"I haven't checked."

"When you get a spare moment, please."

"Let's see 'a spare moment', I'm not sure what that is. A new TV show?" She smiled at him. She enjoyed teasing him with a bit of a flirty edge. He grinned and walked back towards his office. He opened the letter and a sheet of paper was blank except for the words, 'HELL TO PAY' bolded, large font and in all caps. Puzzled and slightly annoyed, he sat down at his computer and pulled up the security video. He ran it backwards until he saw a figure, dressed in black, walk up to the front door. The figure taped the envelope to the door, paused and then turn to the camera. He obviously knew he was being recorded so he quickly turned to the camera, flipped it the bird, and left. Chase slowed the playback speed and in the darkness of the early morning tried to see the face of the hooded figure. He made out that he was wearing a Jigsaw" mask from those Saw movies. "Just a prank," he thought. "Someone's idea of a sick joke. Hopefully." He left the office to stop by the teacher's lounge for coffee. Alma didn't drink coffee and he noticed she already had her herbal tea. "Going for coffee." he said.

"Okay."

First bell had already rung so classes were in session. He had a stash of Keurig cups so he could have French Vanilla whenever he wanted. He met Mr. Sacks in the lounge.

"Morning, Don."

"Morning, Jack. What's the good word?"

"Well next year's budget has been approved. Even with the new school going up."

"That's great!" Don was the biology teacher and had been asking for new equipment for the past 5 years. "New stereoscopes finally?" "Yeah I asked for the electronic ones. They record and store digital video."

"Oh, very cool!" He fist bumped Chase and bounced to class with glee. Chase smiled that he made him happy. They started at Langston High together and they became pretty good friends. He reached up for his box of French Vanilla k-cups and it was empty. He thought he had at least half a box left. He checked the trash and they were there. All hacked up. Why would someone do that? He was really annoyed until he looked in the box and found another note that said, "HELL TO PAY". Now Chase was mad. He was going to find the culprit that seemed to be targeting him directly. He went back to his office.

The rest of the morning was uneventful. After processing paperwork all morning, he looked at the clock and it was almost 11am. He remembered that the Hanney brothers had to be dismissed early. He spoke to Alma. "Alma, have the Hanney boys come down to the office for dismissal, please."

"I just did. They showed up on their own. Their mother was waiting and the left about 5 minutes ago."

"Ah, okay. Lemme know next time, okay?"

"No Sweat."

There was something strange about that whole thing. A little too perfect but not strange enough to spend too much time thinking about it. Lunch was good and the afternoon was quiet.

It was Chase's turn to cover detention after school and he was hoping the kids had been good today. He actually liked detention because he could talk to some kids who may need some fatherly guidance. His own daughter was in college, and he missed having kids at home. Missed his wife too. He was walking to detention when something at the lost and found caught his eye. A textbook with a brown bag cover. The words "HELL TO PAY" were drawn in a gothic, rock and roll style across the front and across the binder. Chase stopped to see who the book belonged to and was surprised to see his own name scrawled across the inside cover, with all the previous owner's names carefully blacked out. Chase took the book and went to detention.

"Anybody know about this?" There were about six kids in detention. Chase held the book up. "Somebody is playing some kind of prank. I would appreciate any info on this."

"It's a local band," A goth girl named Tilda from the back spoke up. A friend of mine is the drummer.

Chase looked at her. "What else can you tell me about this band?"

"They've been playing some parties for the older kids. There are other bands like Vomit, The Butt Scratchers, Terrible Jack and the Dummies, but Hell To Pay is the best."

"Okay, are they kids that go here?"

"Most of them. I think they're all in the school band."

"Okay thanks. Why don't you head out early? A thank you from me. Just stay out of trouble, okay?"

"Sure thing, Mr. Chase." She smiled uncharacteristically and left.

Chase resolved to check in with the music teacher in the morning. "It must be one of the band members trying to make a statement and promote the band." Chase thought as he drove home. He was relieved it wasn't more serious than that. He knew that some kids spent time finding themselves in high school. He chocked it up to an overzealous musician and dismissed it. He went home and Skyped with his daughter, Courtney, at college.

"How are you, Sweetie?"

"Fine, Dad. How are you? How are you feeling? Are you eating?"

"Yes Sweetheart. I am staying on my eating plan. I'm only 10 pounds away from my goal."

"Awesome. So, any prospects?"

"No, I'm not ready yet."

"Dad! It's been 5 years. Mom would not want you to be alone."

"I'm not alone. I have you."

"And you always will-at least until I get married."

"Is there someone you have in mind?"

"No-you know I want to finish school first. Plus, I may do Montreal after."

"Okay. What about Dance Co?"

"Show is in three weeks. You're still coming, right?"

"Wouldn't miss it."

"What about Alma?"

"What about her?"

"Why don't you invite her? You'll have 4 hours in the car to get to know her."

"Would you like that? You always liked her."

"She was really nice to me when Mom died. I was only 15."

"You know her better than I do."

"Well, tell her she's invited by me."

"Okay, I'll see if she's free."

"Cool. I have to go, Dad. The cafe is closing soon and I'm hungry."

"All right Sweetheart. I love you. Watch out for that chili."

"Very funny. Love you too, Dad."

Jack loved his daughter. He was an admitted "overprotective father'. She was beautiful from the day she was born and a joy from day one. Jack enjoyed being a father and husband. Amanda, his wife, was a great mom, despite her difficult upbringing. There was a lot of emotional baggage but she overcame it-at least for a while. When she was diagnosed with Multiple Sclerosis, it affected her resolve and she began to become more difficult. She found out about the MS when Courtney was five and dealt with it the best she could. She endured difficult treatment for about 7 years. Unfortunately, the illness also weakened her immune system and when she caught pneumonia, it made her septic. She lasted about 4 days.

Jack missed his wife. Admittedly he had problems towards the end with her; her attitude was getting pretty bad and they had more of their share of arguments. He knew it was the illness but also it was all the abuse she suffered as a child. Amanda's mother was a textbook hypochondriac and spoiled as a child. It made her a spoiled adult. Jack knew it was important that Amanda and her mother reconcile. He made her see that her mother was not a horrible person, though. She mellowed over time and Amanda got along with her. She enjoyed having a strong, protective son-in-law but was very fussy, and that got on his nerves from time to time. Amanda and her mother had issues and knew how to push each other's buttons. They still cared for each other, but as strained as their relationship was, they still kept in touch and got together on occasion. Amanda usually had to spend the night when she saw her mother because the ride was just long enough to wear her out. That's how MS works. You feel fine until you are tired then it knocks you out for days. Jack hated the disease for that. It was sneaky and dishonest.

Jack logged off of Skype and made himself dinner. He got to be a very good cook since he had to do all the cooking for Amanda. She still considered it her kitchen even though she never used it. He chuckled every time she said that. He sat down to eat and watch his shows. He thought he might go out for a beer but it was a Tuesday so he decided to read and turn in early, instead. He was watching the news when he saw a segment about some graffiti found on a school in Maine. He was lucky that his students were from a decent town. Decent upper-class incomes and parents that took a vested interest in their children's education for the most part. He threw on a movie, dozed off a couple of times and went to bed. It was about 10:30pm.

Jack woke up about 5:30am. He exercised for about 30 minutes, showered and went to school. He greeted Alma as usual. Principal Scarley called him into the office. "What's up Brian?"

"Have you heard of this band, 'Hell to Pay'?"

"As a matter of fact, I just found out about them yesterday. Why?"

"They left a note taped to the front door this morning, or a fan did."

"Weird, someone did the same thing yesterday. They left my name on it."

"Take a look."

Brian handed him an envelope exactly like the one before. Inside a letter size sheet of paper, with "HELL TO PAY" written across the top, and a chilling difference. There were photos of school administration printed on the sheet with red exes across all of them. Even admin staff. "This is bad." Brian was sweating. "I'm calling the police."

"Wait. I think I may know some of the folks in this band. Give me an hour."

"Twenty minutes. I can have my coffee and calm down in that time."

"Alright." Jack walked to the music room and found the music teacher, Gina Schwartz. She was one of Courtney's favorite teachers and they got along well. "Gina, I need to talk to you."

"Hi, Jack, I have a class right now, can it wait?"

"No. It's important."

"Okay, hold on." She gave the attendance sheet to the chorus captain and stepped outside the room. "What's going on?"

"What do you know about this band, 'Hell to Pay'?"

"A couple of my students are in it. I think maybe some older college kids. I encourage outside musical projects. Their music is not my thing, though. Why?"

"We think someone in the band or maybe the whole band is targeting the school. Look at this."

Jack showed her the letter. "Oh my God. This is bad."

"Brian wants to get the police involved but I've asked him to wait until I could get a handle on it. Can you help?"

"Of Course. I will talk to the students in have in the band."

"Okay, keep this under your hat for now, we don't want to start a panic."

"Alright. A couple of them are in this class."

"Okay. I will stall Brian for more time."

Jack walked back to the office and Mrs. Schwartz went in to talk to the band members. He hoped Brian had calmed down enough to wait a while longer before calling the police. He walked into Brian's office. "Weird. The phone's down."

"Just as well. Gina knows some kids in that band. We may have a lead to what's going on."

"Okay, but I have a bad feeling."

"Me too. I will check with Gina in a little while. What's happening with the superintendent?"

"Well she's under investigation. She has a real possibility of being indicted. You can't just hide twenty million dollars and have no one notice."

"Yeah, she had a brilliant career. Too bad. Do you think she did it?"

"After last years' faculty bash at her vacation home? Absolutely. I am sorry she felt she had to do that."

"Well at least the new school is paid for."

"Yeah, but we're going to need that twenty million to run it. Laurie knew that. Let's hope we're all wrong."

Jack knew Superintendent Laurie Clark. She had come from the other side of the state and loved being in Langston. She seemed to live well, even by Superintendent standards. She loved parties and was able to invite faculty and staff without violating any kind of fraternization rules, or so it seemed. Jack figured it was some kind of tax write-off. He went to a few before his wife died then he lost interest. Courtney said he should go to meet women but he thought he wasn't ready yet. She was worried about her father because of her being away at school. She hated the thought of him being alone. Jack loved her for that. "Looking after the old man, that's my girl." He thought. He went back to the music room. He saw Gina and noticed she was visibly upset.

"What's wrong?" Jack asked.

"Well, the kids in that band said they had nothing to do with the letters or any harassment...."

"But?"

"They said they had to kick out two people. Will Turner who was always a hothead, and the other was one of the founding members, Ethan Wass. They said Ethan got really mad, really violent. I knew Ethan-he was a good kid. A talented musician-enough to go professional and I think he was going to apply to Berklee."

"So, would he do something like this?"

"Normally, I'd say no, but since his father walked out on him and his mother and two younger siblings, he changed. He got into goth culture and became very withdrawn. It was last September and he was supposed to graduate this year. He lasted until a few weeks ago and then I haven't seen him. He hasn't shown up to class-I'm not even sure that he's been coming to school at all."

"I'll check the attendance records and see." Jack hurried to the office. "Alma, pull up the attendance record for Ethan Wass."

"That's easy, he quit school two weeks ago."

"That's a shame. Was he eighteen?"

"Yes. There's nothing we can do except invite him back."

"Do you have his number?"

"I'll get it." Alma looked up the number and wrote it on a post it. Jack took the number into his office and closed the door. He knew the land line was down so he used his cell. He dialed and a sleepy voice answered.

"Hello?"

"Hi this is Mr. Chase from Langston High. Is Ethan there?"

"This is Ethan."

"Hey there. I haven't seen you in school for a while. Are you Okay?"

"Yes, I'm fine. Goodbye."

"Wait! Ethan, look I know you've had a rough time and that you are old enough to decide to come back to school or not. If you need to talk, or help or anything you can call me okay? Even if it's just to talk."

There was a long pause. A sniffle, then a "Thank you." Jack wanted to plead with him to come back to school but he held his breath. "I'll think about it. I gotta go." The phone went silent and Jack hung up. It always broke his heart a little when a kid quit school. He had pushed his open-door policy so kids could come to him and not feel self-conscious. He didn't have the chance to talk to Ethan and wished he had. As he was pondering his next move, Scarley came into his office. "She's been indicted. I just got the e-mail."

"Oooh that's going to hurt. It'll be bad publicity for the town."

"I know. I'm thinking maybe we should have a school assembly to do damage control for the students."

"I think that's a good idea." Scarley's phone rang. It was the DPW about the land lines. It seemed that it was vandalism and that the damage was pretty extensive. Someone knew how to knock out the phones for a day or two. It was almost dismissal time so Jack went out to meet the buses. Once that was done, he went back and spoke with Alma.

"My daughter's dance show is this weekend. She mentioned she'd like you to come with me to see her. Would you like to go?"

"Sure, what time?"

"Well we could leave Saturday morning and stop for coffee. It's about a two-hour ride and there's a cute little eatery/antique shop in Erving on the way. Say around 10:30?"

"Sure, it's a date!" She seemed exciting about going. Jack was pleased about Alma going and began to look at her a little differently. He collected his stuff to go home and thought about texting Courtney to tell her. "Nah, I'll surprise her that'll be more fun," he thought. It was a Friday night so traffic was a little heavier. He arrived home and instinctively checked his phone. Scarley had called and left a message.

"Jack, this is Brian. Something very bad has happened. The Hanney Boys are missing. They were at the funeral yesterday and after they had come home the mother brought them to their grandparents. They just found them-the grandparents are dead and the boys gone. Call me."

"How horrible," Jack thought. "I hope they are okay." He speed-dialed Scarley.

"Hey. I just got your message. What happened?"

"The Hanney Boys were sent to their grandparents house after the funeral. The mother wanted to visit with some friends after the funeral and I guess she wanted the boys to be with family. When she came back to pick them up, the place was crawling with police, and the elderly couple were dead. Shot multiple times."

"Dear Lord. No sign of the boys?"

"Well if there's a good part, then that's probably it. The grandparents were the only deaths."

"Okay what do we do about that?"

"Well, we were going to have the assembly about Laurie, I guess we will need to add this. Man, I had no idea I would ever have to do something like this!"

"I hear ya. I'll make some notes for the assembly. Try and get some sleep."

"Yeah I'll try."

Jack hung up the phone. He thought about dinner but he didn't feel hungry yet. He sat down on the couch and just pondered the situation. There was a pounding at the door and he opened it.

There stood Ethan Wass, bloodied and wheezing.

"Ethan! What are you doing here?

"I tried to stop them. They took those boys!!"

"Who did? Come inside!"

Ethan was visibly upset. For a split second, Jack wondered if he actually was leaving those notes at school. He put that out of his head.

"Start from the beginning. What happened?"

"I was coming home from the skate park. I saw the Hanney boys playing outside. A van pulled up with two guys and shoved them in a van. One guy pulled out a machine gun and went into the house. There were shots and a lot of screaming. I tried to get the boys out of the van but the other guys beat me. I got a few shots in but he was pretty big."

"You could have been killed! Did you call the police?"

"No, I had a few run ins with them over the past few weeks at the skate park. They said if I caused any more trouble, they'd arrest me and put me in jail."

"Okay, I'll go to bat for you with the police. It was good you came to me, Ethan. Let's call them and we'll get you cleaned up."

Jack dialed 911 and told them about Ethan. He brought Ethan into the kitchen and got out hydrogen peroxide and some cloths. The police came over. It was a small town so most people knew the officers on the force. Officer Jerry Riggs showed up at the door. Riggs was one of Jack's students a few years ago when he was still teaching in a classroom.

"Hi Mr. Chase. What's the trouble?"

"This young man saw and tried to stop the Hanney boys from being kidnapped." Ethan was reluctant to come forward and talk to Riggs. When Riggs saw Ethan, he frowned. "Ethan and I have met. A lot, lately it seems. So, what's the deal?"

"I saw the guys who took those boys and killed that couple."

"Okay we'll need to go over to Forestville to talk to the sketch artist. But I warn you, if you're lying to me."

"Why the hell would I lie about something like that? You're a jerk!" Ethan was defensive.

"Calm down, Ethan. Jerry, I think he's telling the truth. He was pretty banged up when he got here."

"Ok, Mr. Chase. I'll take your word on it. Come on, Wass."

"Make sure he gets home safe too, please?"

"Sure thing."

Jack looked at Ethan. "You did the right thing, Ethan. I am proud of you." Ethan seemed to perk up a bit and left with Riggs. Jack took a moment and called Scarley. He told him what happened and how Ethan was heroic in trying to save those boys. Questions remained that bothered him. Jack got a notebook and sat down. He started writing questions down. Why were the boys kidnapped and not killed? Why did they kill the grandparents? Who took the boys and the wanted the grandparents dead? Would there be a ransom? Jack had a process to figure out problems. If he wrote the questions down and let them sit, his brain would begin to come up with answers. Plus having them 'out of his head' eased his mind.

He looked at the clock and felt tired. He had not eaten yet so he warmed up the food he made, stayed up for another hour after and went to bed about midnight.

He woke up about 9am. It was Saturday and he figured a trip to Courtney's college would clear his head. He had cereal, checked his e-mail as he ate, showered, and called Alma.

"We still on?"

"Absolutely. It's a nice day for a drive."

"Perfect! I'll see you in about an hour."

Jack hung up the phone and got dressed. He enjoyed a ride out to western Massachusetts especially this time of year. Fall foliage was in full swing and North Hoosac was beautiful. It was on the other side of the Berkshire Mountains and was a leisurely ride. Jack picked up Alma and they got to the highway. "Did you hear about what happened yesterday?"

"The Hanney Boys? Yes, Brian called me.

"Ethan Wass tried to save them."

"Really?"

"Yeah. He's a real hero. He came over my house to tell me. He was pretty banged up. Once he told me, I called the police. Apparently, Ethan's had a few run ins."

"Wow. Ethan's always been a good kid-at least up until his father left."

"I think he came to me I think because I called him yesterday. I reached out to him. I hope it was enough."

"It seemed like it if he came to you."

Jack smiled at the thought that he may have gotten through to Ethan. He thought he should call Brian to see if there had been any changes. He waited until they stopped in Erving for coffee.

"Hey Brian, any updates?

"Yeah they arrested Ethan Wass in connection to the kidnapping."
"What? Ethan came to me last night. He said he tried to help those boys
and had the bruises and bloody nose to show for it."

"I'm not sure what he told you but they've identified one of the kidnappers as Ethan's father."

"Crap. Okay, so what are they charging him with?"

"Accessory to kidnapping and accessory to murder of Mr. and Mrs.
Christensen."

"Where is he now?"

"Worcester County Jail, up in Wachusett."

"Okay thanks, keep me posted. I'm going to my daughter's recital so
text me."

Jack hung up the phone. He walked over to Alma who was sipping
coffee as she browsed antiques. "Ethan's been arrested."

"What? Why?"

"They think he was helping the kidnappers and the murder."

"Oh, my that's awful! I never pictured Ethan able to do anything like
that. I just can't believe it."

"I really don't believe it either."

Jack and Alma were uncomfortably quiet for a while in the car. "Do
you think he had anything to do with it?" Alma asked.

"No. I really don't." Jack was bothered by this development. "He was
exhausted and upset when he came to me. You can't really lie about
something when you're like that."

"I suppose. What are you going to do?"

"Not sure. I really want to help Ethan. I can really figure it out until I talk to him."

Alma wasn't sure if she should ask any more questions so she changed the subject.

"So how long til we get there?

"About 25 minutes. We're at the top of the mountain range so we're almost there."

"Did I read that sign right? We're in Florida?"

"Yessir! Florida, Mass. Back 200 years ago some doctor settled here. They say it was created around the same time of the Spanish American war and that Florida was the reason or something like that. Anyway, not much here."

"Windmills, and a decent view."

"Yeah." Jack chuckled and forgot things for a short while. They came down the other side of the mountain. They came through the famous "Hairpin Turn" on Route 2 and continued into North Hoosac. It was a typical New England town, although it had a small, public college. It boasted an art museum, the Massachusetts Museum of Contemporary Art, or Mass MOCA for short. It is the largest museum of contemporary art in the entire country. It was put into a former textile mill that had been an electronics factory from the end of World War II to the mid 1980's. It was a huge place. The show was on the main stage at the museum. Jack and Alma didn't have time to meet Courtney before the show so they planned to go to dinner afterwards. There was a popular place called the Freight Yard Bar and Grille over by the tracks. They had gone there before and the food was very good.

They parked and went in. Jack was hoping he could enjoy the show despite the kidnapping incident. He was truly concerned about the Hanney Boys and Ethan. The show was fantastic. Courtney danced her heart out as usual and the college students were all amazing. Once the show ended, they went out to the lobby to mix and mingle with the other parents. Courtney's roommate and best friend, Brittany Westinghouse was in the last routine. We met her parents in the lobby. Jack introduced Alma and they chatted. The girls came out after they had changed.

"Would you care to join us for dinner? We're going to the Freight Yard."

"Actually, we are going to Pittsfield. We have family there and we made plans," Mrs. Westinghouse said.

"Oh okay, enjoy your evening." Jack was actually relieved to have Courtney to himself. They went to the restaurant and ordered.

"That was a great show, Sweetheart. You guys worked really hard."

"Thanks, Dad. We had fun."

"I've never seen anything like that. Very cool!" Alma seemed glad to be involved in the family dynamic. "I used to dance in college. It was a lot more traditional."

"Thanks, Alma. We do two shows a year-the first before Christmas Break and then a Springtime Gala." Courtney said. "It's a lot of work but fun."

"And quite a commitment." Jack added.

"Well, you only live once." Courtney added. Their appetizers were steaming but smelling delicious. "So, what had been going on at school?"

Jack had put it out of his head. Everything came rushing back. "Well, not good things."

"What happened?"

"The Hanney boys have been kidnapped, their grandparents murdered and Ethan Wass has been arrested for his alleged involvement."

"Oh my God, Dad! I knew Ethan. I tutored him in music! He's very talented."

"He quit school after his father left the family. I invited him back to school and tried to let him know we cared about him. He came to the house last night and said he tried to stop the kidnapping. Had the wounds to prove it too."

"Wow, wow." Courtney was speechless. She savored a mozzarella stick and thought. "Do you think he had anything to do with it?", she asked.

"No, Sweetie. I really don't. I think he was telling the truth."

Alma spoke up. "I can't really see him doing it either. I just don't think he has it in him." Jack changed the subject.

So, when are you bringing Derek back for a visit?"

"Soon, Dad, soon. He's in New York interviewing for a design job."

Jack smiled and said with mock sternness, "Don't go moving off to New York now!"

"Dad! I still have another year of school!" Everyone laughed and they enjoyed the rest of the evening.

They went back to Courtney's dorm and visited a little longer. It got to be 9pm and Jack thought he should get back. He hated leaving his little girl although she wasn't so little anymore. He'd see her in two weeks for Thanksgiving break so he could deal until then. He and Alma each said goodbye and headed back to Langston. Jack was quiet for a while. He needed to talk to stay awake on the two-hour drive home so he figured he could brainstorm with Alma.

"What do you know about Ethan's father?"

"As I remember him, he was kind of rough around the edges. Always in jeans and either in a truck in the winter time or on his Harley in the warmer weather. In the summer, I'd run into him at Peach Hill Farm for ice cream now and then. Not the warm and fuzzy type but he seemed to be a decent father. At least until he left."

"Huh, okay. What about the Hanney boys? Did you know their father?"

"No, I never met him always just dealt with the mother. I would see her working at the Town Hall for a while. Don't know if she still works there."

This gave Jack a lot to think about. Was there another connection between Ethan and the Hanney boys? What was it? He got the idea to check the town hall and even check public records. He and Alma drove through the winding part of Route 2 where it met up with I-91 and skirted the outer edge of Greenmont, Mass. It was another hour and they stopped to stretch their legs and use the bathroom. The rest of the trip they talked about the things they had in common. Finally, Jack drove up to Alma's apartment building and they stopped. Jack, being a gentleman, walked Alma to the door.

"So," Alma began, "Is this going to be a regular thing?"

"Well, I'd like it to be. Courtney thinks I need someone."

"She's a bright girl, and she's right. But if this is going anywhere, we need some ground rules since we work together."

"Ok. I think that's a good idea."

"First, work stays professional. Nothing is worse than gossip with high schoolers"

"Agreed. We don't want another fiasco like a few years ago with those two teachers caught in the chemistry closet."

"Second, we should date out of sight as much as possible. So, we might need to find stuff at home to do, or out of town."

Jack pulls her close. "I can think of a few things to do at home."

Alma smiled. "Me too. But we should go slow. I don't have a good track record with relationships."

"No worries. It's been a while so I'm rusty myself. I haven't dated anyone in over twenty years."

"I understand. It'll be fun. No pressure, no worries."

"Deal." They share a wonderfully innocent kiss and parted ways. Jack had that warm feeling that he missed for a long time. It was nice.

Jack slept well and later than he planned. He thought about going to church as he hadn't been in a while, but decided to take a rest day. He checked the DVR and saw it was at about 80% full. He was actually glad to have a variety of movies and shows to watch, but he checked the weather first. He checked the news and his mood changed. Channel 5 News had come out from Boston to cover the kidnapping. Now everyone knew and damage control was going to be even harder. The phone rang. It was Scarley.

"Are you seeing this?"

"Yeah I just turned it on. Who leaked this?"

"I don't know. This is a nightmare."

"We'll still need to do the assembly, now more than ever. Suggestions?"

"Keep it simple. Assure that everyone is safe at the school. Maybe talk to the police to have an officer around, just to make people feel safe. We don't know how this is going to go."

"Ok good stuff. Let's touch base first thing in the morning."

"Will do."

Jack dreaded Monday morning but tried to get back to the restful mood. He watched a movie, but his mind was on the Hanney Boys. He went out for a walk to get some air and decided to see Ethan at the station. He found out that they sent him to Devens for holding until they can bring formal charges. He pondered how he could help Ethan as he walked home. He decided to do a little detective work after school on Monday. He'd start by going to see Ethan's mother.

Monday morning came and Jack went to school a little early. Scarley arrived at the same time. They strategized about the assembly and decided on what to say and how to say it. They were on their way to the assembly when Laurie Clark showed up. Scarley and Jack both looked at each other and secretly decided they would not mention the indictment. They would just focus on the kidnapping.

"So, what's the plan, Boys?" They both hated the insincere way she carried herself. She was a shady politician with a teaching degree and enough certifications to fill the position. She apparently charmed the town selectmen and enjoyed the status of her position. Most of the faculty just put up with her; few are actually friendly with her and most of the time she seemed genuinely interested in doing her job, but it always masked an underlying ambition to move upward in her field. Her appearance at the assembly made things a hundred times harder.

"Well Brian and I-

Laurie puffed out her chest. "Tell you what, I'll take point and deal with this kidnapping situation. You guys just stand there and look pretty."

"Laurie that's a bad idea. Jack and I have worked out what we were-"

"That's DOCTOR Clark, Brian at least when we are out of the office. She swept by the two frustrated men and onto the auditorium stage. After several moments of microphone adjustment and feedback, she addressed the student body. "Students, faculty, and staff, thank you for taking this time to get the real story on this horrible event! Let me first assure you that everyone is safe here at Langston High School. For those of you that have younger sibling in the other schools, Turkey Hill Middle School and Langston Primary School, you are safe here. I personally guarantee it. Now for the details of what happened. Many of you know the Hanney Brothers, Johnny, Bobby, and Matthew, and know that they have been kidnapped. We know that they will be okay and will be back with us soon. The young man responsible is a former student of Langston High. A young man our administration has failed because he left school for a life of crime. His name is, "

Jack cringed, Scarley covered his mouth, not sure to go interrupt Clark or brace for impact. Before he could act, she uttered his name.

"Ethan Wass!"

The crowd gasped as she uttered the alleged villain's name. "Ethan was a good student here at Langston until tragedy struck. His father abandoned him and he turned to a life of crime. We are expecting a ransom note from his partners at any moment. Ethan is in custody, and we will bring his accomplices to justice. Thank you. You are dismissed back to your classes."

Jack was horrified. Scarley looked like he was going to throw up. Clark walked quickly up the aisle towards the back of the auditorium. Jack and Scarley walked fast down the hall to try to intercept her. Jack grabbed her arm and ushered her into the office. "DO YOU KNOW WHAT YOU'VE DONE??? ARE YOU MAD???"

"You will not use that tone with me, Mr. Chase!" Clark was indignant.

"You had no right to say any of that! This entire district is a powder keg and you just lit the match!!!"

"Mr. Chase, I've said what needed to be said. Be careful, I'm still the Superintendent and I still control your job!" She turned on her heel and walked out of the office. Jack knew she wouldn't listen to anything he said. Jack and Scarley retreated to Scarley's office.

"She has created a monster. The students, the staff are all scared." Scarley was exasperated.

Jack was frustrated. "Plus, that Wass kid doesn't stand a chance." He added.

"I know." Scarley was genuinely concerned about Ethan. "We have to get to the bottom of this thing. The Hanney boys' and Ethan's lives are on the line." Jack knew their attempt at damage control was a failure. Clark's interference created more fear and dissention all through the district.

"So, what do we do?" Scarley was scratching his head.

"After school, I'm going to go talk to his mother. Maybe I can get some kind of information about Ethan that can help him."

"Good luck. Let me know if I can help." Jack spent the rest of the day calming students and conferring with faculty. Finally, he got his bus duty covered and left school just as the final bell rang. He decided to start at the Town Hall. He did not know if Ethan's mom still worked there. He stopped at the Town Manager's office to find out. He spoke with the administrative assistant at the window.

"Hello. I'm not sure if she still works here but I'm looking for Martha Wass." She was young enough to be one of Jack's students, but he did not recognize her.

"She still works for the town. She's the admin down at the DPW on Route 13."

"Would she still be there? I need to speak with her."

"She should be. Her hours are until 4pm."

"Okay thank you very much."

Jack drove over to the DPW garage. He wasn't sure what would happen but maybe he'd be able to make sense of this mess. He parked and went into the office. They had renovated the building a few years ago and made the office area very nice. He felt he was walking into a corporate office. The reception desk was round and large. It looked like a spaceship. Behind it sat an attractive, well-groomed woman. "I'm looking for Martha Wass."

"You've found her. What can I do for you?"

"My name is Jack Chase. I'm the vice principal at the high school."

"You're Mr. Chase? Ethan talked about you. You invited him back to school."

"Yes, I did. He came to me after he tried to help the Hanney boys. I tried to help him but I'm not sure if I did or not."

"You said he tried to help those boys. Does that mean you think he's innocent?"

"Yes, Mrs. Wass. I do. But I need to find out what happened up to the incident. I'd like to ask you some questions at the risk of being indelicate."

"Right now, my head is spinning. They didn't want me to come to work. They said I could have paid leave but I told them I'd use it later. If I stayed home, I would have gone nuts. Please, ask away."

"When exactly did Ethan's father leave?"

"Mid-August. He was a trucker. He wasn't warm and fuzzy except when it came to Ethan."

"Really?"

"Yes, he loved Ethan. He hated to leave him but he couldn't find work anywhere else. He was getting ready to get a job that would have him home most nights."

"I see. You guys were getting along?"

"Sure, other than him being gone a lot. We had a few arguments about it but nothing really bad. When he left, he said he needed time to think about things. He did that every so often, but he always came back.

He'd only be gone a few hours when he was like that. He came from a pretty abusive family so he didn't want his family to suffer like he did."

"He never hit you?"

"No."

"But he just left."

"Yes, I thought he would come back but it's been 2 months."

"Did you file a missing person's report?"

"No, when he left, he was pretty angry. He said some things, I said some things. It was pretty bad."

"Just about his job? There was nothing else you fought about?"

"Well, there is one thing. It's kind of our family secret. You see, everyone thought he came from a poor background. In reality, his family is very wealthy. His father was a high-powered executive with a lot a political connections." She paused to ponder her next words, "and let's just say his share of companions, to put it nicely. Mark hated the way he treated his mother. His mother was very kind and good to him. She was no saint but she was faithful at least. About a year after we were married, Mark and his father had a major blow out. It was so bad that Mark's father disowned him and cut him out of the family fortune. It was a major blow since Mark didn't go to college and was expected to take over the family business. His father, despite his shortcomings, was very concerned about his image. A son with no ambition and skill was an embarrassment. Mark was a hard worker, always had been but he wanted to work on cars and motorcycles. His father thought that was beneath him. Mark also called his father on his dalliances and the treatment of his mother. His father couldn't handle it and kicked him out. He also blackballed Mark from every ivy league and even decent sized public colleges. Mark would have the last laugh because he ended up going to a technical school which is what he wanted anyway. For a while, we struggled. His mother helped us secretly but had to be careful his that father didn't find out. Small sums of money and things. Then, right when Mark was about to graduate, his mom died. Car accident. Mark investigated somewhat and never believed it was accidental and held his father responsible. He was never the same after that. They haven't spoken since."

"Wow, that is some story." Jack was amazed. Martha continued.

"Yes, well there's one more thing. One of Mark's father's companions was Maribeth Hanney."

Jack stopped dead for a second. "You mean that Ethan and the Hanney brothers…"

"Are blood related." Martha continued.

"I have to ask, do any of them know?" Jack was still trying to process.

"Ethan knows. Once it was all out in the open, we decided along with Ethan that the boys were too young to understand the situation and that once they got older, we would tell them. We tried to pass them off as cousins, but Maribeth and I had trouble getting along. I don't hold anything against her, we were just too damaged by the whole thing."

"Martha, thank you for enlightening me. Take my cell number and call me if you think of anything else that may help. I'll let you know if I find anything out."

"Thank you, Mr. Chase. Please if you can help Ethan out of this mess, I would…" She started to tear up. Jack felt for her. "Martha, I will do everything I can to help Ethan. I promise."

"Thanks." Jack left the office, thinking about his next move. He was still reeling from the conversation he just had with Martha Wass. Ethan and the Hanney boys are blood relatives-cousins. He had uncovered a long-standing family scandal and now he had to figure out what it had to do with the kidnapping. He went to his car and got his notebook out. He started writing the questions down. What did the Wass family problems have to do with the kidnapping? Why were the boys kidnapped and why hasn't there been a ransom demand made? Are the boys even still alive? The next step was to find Maribeth Hanney. Jack got the address and went to the Hanney home. They lived in a small house in the Whalom section of town, by the lake. Years ago, there had been a lot of summertime activity due to Whalom Park. A popular local attraction, it was an old amusement park that had been around for over 100 years. The park had been shut down in 2000 due to serious disagreements within the family that owned it. The squabbling had resulted in the park being shut down, dismantled and the assets sold off. The land was eventually sold to developers and new, luxury condos were built in its place. Jack pulled onto Florence Street and parked. It was a small, cramped house, but in a decent neighborhood. Several of the houses in the area had been seasonal cabins. This one was winterized and then a second floor added, giving it a somewhat misshapen look. There was a late model sedan in the two-car parking space. Jack approached the door. It opened before he could press the bell and an attractive woman in her late 30s answered the door. "Are you the detective?"

"No Ma'am, my name is Jack Chase, I'm the vice principal..." She cut him off. "Yes Mr. Chase I recognize you now. Forgive me."

"You must be Mrs. Hanney. I completely understand. May I speak with you?"

"Yes of course, come in please." Jack followed her in. The house was clean but cluttered with mail and official looking paperwork. Jack noticed the name Benjamin Wasserstein on multiple documents and mail. He knew of Wasserstein. He was a wealthy local businessman with not the best reputation. Jack put a couple of details together. Maribeth fussed around in the kitchen. "Can I get you a drink, Mr. Chase?"

"No thank you. How are you holding up?"

"Not well I'm afraid. I'm worried about my boys."

"I can only imagine what you are going through. I am trying to find them and help Ethan Wass. We don't think he had anything to do with the kidnapping. As a matter of fact, he tried to save the boys."

"I was surprised to hear that he was arrested for his involvement. My boys and Ethan were friends. He was like a big brother to them." She was tired but still very worried about her sons. Jack used the most compassionate tone he could muster. "I know this may seem a strange question but do you know of anyone who would want to harm you or the boys?"

"Not to my knowledge. We aren't wealthy people."

"Did you know Ethan's grandfather?" Maribeth was surprised at the question, but answered softly.

"Yes, I did. I used to work for him."

"What did you do for him?"

"Administrative stuff, mostly. I was his executive assistant for three years. He offered a lot of benefits. Even paid off my school loans. It helped me buy this house."

"Mrs. Hanney, please understand that I am only trying to get to the bottom of this so I need to ask some difficult questions. Were you and Mr. Wasserstein having an affair?" She paused for a moment. Jack didn't know if he crossed a line or if she actually had feelings for him. "Yes, we did. You have to understand that he was a very powerful man and I was for lack of a better term, poor as a church mouse. Once I started working for him, we would work long nights. He started to confide in me about his marital troubles and how his wife cheated on him and how badly she treated him. I bought the whole story and even thought I could be the woman he needed. I even started thinking that I was in love with him. As you can guess, one thing led to another and we began an affair. It lasted about four years."

"Long enough to have three children with him."

"Yes. My sons' father is Benjamin Wasserstein."

"I'm sorry. It must be very hard for you."

"Not financially. You see, after two years, everyone pretty much knew we were sleeping together. He hadn't divorced his wife as he promised me and things at the office were getting harder and harder to handle. Finally, when I was about eight months pregnant with my youngest, Virginia Wasserstein paid me a visit. I had already purchased this house and living here a short time and she knocked on my door. I was scared but I invited her in. She came in. I didn't know if she knew about me and her husband. That question was answered pretty fast. She had three large envelopes, each with a woman's name on it, one with mine. She opened one and showed me pictures of her husband and another woman. She even had a newspaper in some shots to prove when it was taken. She reached for another envelope and the same thing was there. Ben and a different woman. The third one had my name on it and as you have probably already guessed, it was pictures of me and Ben."

"Is it safe to assume he was seeing all three of you at the same time?" Jack was more than a little disgusted.

"Yes. I was seeing Ben and he was seeing these other women at the same time. Virginia explained that she had hired a private investigator to follow her husband. She also explained that these were his 'local' girls and that he had several more all over the country. He preferred having women he employed. It was a power thing. She also told me that he cannot divorce her due to the prenuptial agreement they signed when they got married. Without this evidence over him, if they divorced, she would lose everything. If they stayed married then she would have access to all their assets, but she couldn't take any money and leave him. There is a fidelity clause but she said to Ben it was a formality. He could cheat on her and still have enough power over her to keep her from leaving. She said it would make him look better to have a long marriage. But then she said something I didn't expect. Something very strange."

Jack was intrigued. "What was it?"

"She said that she was as trapped as he was because of the pre-nup. She had always been wealthy and that she didn't have a way to support herself if she lost everything. Even with the evidence of cheating, if she divorced him, he could tie the money up for years. He kept her pretty isolated so she really didn't have any marketable skills. She would either be alone in her marriage, or struggling to move past it."

"He created a real mess, didn't he?" Jack said.

"Yes, well a couple of weeks after that, she died in that car accident. Everyone in the company said it was awfully convenient. After the funeral, I went to go see him at the office. I went to the front desk and my security card had been shut off, all of my desk belongings were in a box, and he refused to see me. He had his cell phone shut off but I think he did that for all of the used-up mistresses he had. All I had to show for it was this house. Before Ben dumped me, I made double payments and saved a lot of the money I made so I was okay for a while. Once I had my baby, I took some time and found another job. I can't help thinking that I was one of the lucky ones."

"You may have been, by the sound of it. Do you know anything about Mark Wass?"

"Mark? Yes. Once he and Ben had had a falling out, he was so mad he had his name changed. His real name is…."

"Mark Wasserstein. I had a feeling."

"Do you think any of this can help me get my boys back?" Maribeth's voice had a glimmer of hope. Jack felt bad for her. "I am going to try. You wouldn't happen to have those pictures, would you?"

"No. Virginia took them with her. She said they were her only insurance."

"Insurance against what?"

"If I had to guess, it would have been her death, but it didn't work."

"True, true. Thank you so much for your time. I know this wasn't easy but I promise I will do everything I can to get the boys back."

"Please contact me if you hear anything."

"I will."

Jack left the house feeling sorry for Maribeth. He had to fix this situation. It was almost dinner time but he had one last idea. He would talk to Officer Riggs and find out why Ethan was arrested. He was annoyed that Riggs arrested him instead of bringing him home like he had asked. He headed over to the police station on Mass Ave. Riggs was just finishing his shift when Jack pulled up. "Hey Jerry! Wait up." Jack rushed over to Rigg's car."

"Hey Mr. Chase."

"What happened with Ethan? Why was he arrested?"

"That's an active investigation, Mr. Chase. I'm afraid I can't-"

Jack cut him off. "Jerry! Don't you dare pull that crap on me. You owe me. I never thought I'd have to call that favor, but kid's lives are on the line."

"Okay, Okay. I can't tell you much but someone filed charges against him. When we left your place, we got to the station, I took his statement and my sergeant saw that it was him. When we ran his name through the system, a warrant for his arrest was issued an hour beforehand."

"And this didn't strike you as strange?"

"Well, yeah. It was a crazy coincidence. We've never had a warrant happen so fast and so clean."

"Who issued the warrant?" Jack asked.

"It came from county. I'll have to go back in to look up the judge who signed it."

"All right. Keep this on the down low for now. Do it first thing in the morning and give me a call on my cell."

"Okay, but when this is done, we are even, deal?"

"Deal. And thanks."

Jack pulled into his yard. It had been a hard day. It reminded him of his old army days as a CID investigator. He thought about some of the cases he investigated and how much he enjoyed it. Then he remembered why he retired. Too many bodies. Too many dead children. He was investigating several murders in the Dhi Qar Province. His base was with the 972nd MPs at Camp Adder, Tallil Airbase, located about 5 miles outside of An Nasiriyah, Iraq. It was suspected that some US Marines had gone rogue and laid waste to a village, Lieutenant Calley style. Gruesome. The investigation was difficult and long but in the end it was fruitful. The Marines were found innocent; some Al Qaida sympathizers tried to frame them. Those monsters slaughtered their own people, even family members. But it was the small bodies, the ones that were sacrificed for an evil cause, that soured Jack's soul. He felt something break that day. Once his tour was done, he came back stateside, stayed long enough to earn a retirement and came home. It was part of the reason he went into teaching. By teaching and caring for children, he could cleanse his heart of the images of those Iraqi kids he couldn't save. Now he had to save Ethan and the Hanney boys. He had to.

Jack had just got into the door when Alma called him. "You busy?"

"Just got home. Playing detective all afternoon."

"Perfect. I have some leftovers. I can bring them over."

Jack was relieved he didn't have to make dinner. "Awesome, thanks. That'd be great."

"See you soon." Alma seemed very happy to bring him food. "She's a great lady," Jack thought. He went in and fell onto the couch. After dozing for a few minutes, he decided to check his e-mail. Nothing of any importance. He then looked up Benjamin Wasserstein. He was in his mid-60s, but tan and in good shape. He had a dubious reputation both personally and professionally. Is he capable of murder? Extortion and kidnapping? How and why would he frame a young boy like Ethan? Why would he kill the Christensen's? His phone rang again. It was Scarley.

"Hey Brian. Any news?"

"Yes, there's been a break in the case."

"That's great! What is it?"

"They found the youngest Hanney boy." Jack's heart jumped into his throat. He was hoping for a miracle. "Where?"

"Wandering up New West Townsend Rd. Someone heard him crying and took him in. They recognized him from the news and called the police."

"Oh, thank God. That's great news. I've been doing a little digging and this thing is a lot more complex than we thought. I will fill you in tomorrow. I just got home and Alma's bringing dinner."

"Okay. You guys have been spending a lot of time together."

"Well yeah. We're taking it slow."

"That's good. You two need someone. Hope it works out."

"Thanks, Brian. I'll see you tomorrow."

Jack hung up as Alma knocked and came in. "Hope you're hungry. It's lasagna."

"Oh yeah!" It was obvious that this wasn't leftovers and Jack was very flattered she made a fuss over him. "It's been a long time", Jack thought. "I've been doing some digging. Quite a rock I've turned over and it goes all the up to the famous Ben Wasserstein."

"Wasserstein? I used to work for him. Briefly. I left when he made some very inappropriate comments and advances. He did it to me and pretty much anything female. He got nasty when I said I wasn't interested. I figured I'd leave before I got fired. He was a real creep."

"So, I've gathered. From what I've found out, other girls weren't so lucky to escape. The Hanney Boys? Wasserstein's their father. Once he found out he kicked them out and abandoned them. I think this has something to do with the kidnapping."

"Wow, if it does this could take Wasserstein down, hard."

"You know, you just gave me an idea. With his wife dead, his oldest son missing and his grandchildren out of the way, no one stands to get his money if he dies. It's like he's eliminating his heirs, but why?"

"The only reason to eliminate your heirs would be to either keep the money for yourself or assign another heir." Alma was a great sounding board. She was spot on about Wasserstein.

"We just need to find out why he would change his heirs." They ate and discussed the situation further. They cuddled on the couch for a while and they started to fall asleep. It was almost midnight when they woke up. "Did you want to spend the night? It's pretty late." Jack asked, innocently. "I mean to sleep."

"Uh-huh." Alma was groggy and sprawled on the couch after Jack got up. She fell back to sleep and he covered her with a blanket. He kissed her on the forehead and looked at her for a while. It had been awhile since a woman has been in his apartment. He remembered being married and how he enjoyed the family life. He was rather prudish when it came to things like this. He would let her sleep and let things develop on their own.

Jack woke up at the usual 6am alarm. He smelled bacon and eggs cooking and then coffee. He thought he was dreaming for a moment and then remembered Alma had spent the night. He got up and greeted his new chef. "Wow, it's been awhile since anyone made me breakfast. And on a school day! What a treat!"

"I figured since I fell asleep on you last night, it was the least I could do." Alma had her hair up and face washed. "I hope you didn't mind. I used the face cleaner in the bathroom."

"No problem. It doesn't get used much by me." Jack responded.

"Oh! Oh, I'm so sorry."

"It's okay. The truth is I forgot it was there. If you like it you can have it. Or leave it here for the next time."

"Thanks. So, breakfast is ready."

"Beautiful. Let's eat."

They enjoyed breakfast and each got ready for work. They brought two cars to work but it seemed that it going to be a short-lived activity. Scarley greeted them as they entered the school. "You need to see this," he said. "Clark must have some powerful friends." He pointed to his computer screen which had the Channel 5 News playing on it. The broadcast was on Clark's indictment. She was standing next to the governor at the state house and waving as if she had just been elected. "Chet Boyd, Channel 5 news. Our top story-the indictment of Langston School Superintendent Laurie Clark has been suspended for further investigation. She will remain in her current position until the investigation is concluded. In a related story, a positive turn in the Langston kidnapping of three young boys. The youngest one has been rescued. We were able to speak to Laurie Clark about the details. Heather?"

"Thanks Chet. This is Heather Unger for 5 News. We're here with Laurie Clark, the Langston School District Superintendent. Ms. Clark, what can you tell us?"

"It's DOCTOR Clark, Heather. I can't believe our luck. I was driving down the street towards my home and I saw this poor, young, disheveled boy walking around in a daze. I instantly recognized him as little Billy Hanney, the youngest of the boys who were kidnapped. I stopped to help him and I brought him immediately to the hospital."

"That's great, Dr. Clark. Did he say anything? Does he know where his brothers are?"

"No, he hasn't said a word since I found him. It's been traumatic for him, I'm sure he'll speak after some treatment."

"There you have it. One of the Hanney boys recovered by a heroic educator. Back to you, Chet."

Jack was disgusted. "I suppose we shouldn't be surprised."

Scarley responded, "I don't know how she does it. She can wreck a situation, or make a bad situation worse and she can still make herself out to be a hero. That is one hell of a coincidence."

"You got that right. So, what can we do about here?" Jack mused.

Scarley paced. "The one good thing is that finding Billy may put people a little more at ease. But we still need to find the older boys."

"I-we have a theory on that. Let me get you up to speed on some things, first."

Jack presented his theory about why the boys were kidnapped. "So why would Benjamin Wasserstein want to find a new heir?"

"We don't know that yet. I need to talk to him."

"Take the rest of the day. I need to work damage control here. Alma would you help me?"

"Sure."

"Jack, let me know if you need anything."

"I may need a backstory to get in to see Wasserstein. I'll call you."

"Keep me posted."

This felt like his old CID days. He really wanted to save those boys. He just hoped he wouldn't see any more dead children. He looked up Wasserstein's office address and headed there. He thought it would be in Boston but strangely enough it was only a few miles away on Devens. Devens used to be Fort Devens, an active duty Army post. Jack did a lot of intelligence training there in the late 1980's. He always tried to get permanent party there, and would have if he had stayed in another 5 years. He did not want to drag his family around, plus when his wife was diagnosed with her illness, it made sense to retire. He enjoyed some benefits on Devens, since they kept a small area active in order to support the National Guard and Army Reserve. It was called the "Enclave" and behind the gate was a military clothing store and a small shoppette. The rest of the post was renovated for businesses, manufacturing, pharmaceuticals and some startups. There was a Job Corps facility near the old main gate and the neighboring towns of Nashoba Village and Squannacook support the now heavily ex-military population.

Jack drove past the Enclave and continued down Jackson Rd. He remembered where the Red Cross Building used to be as he turned onto Barnum Rd. The Wasserstein Company was down on the right. It was set far off the road and the grounds were well groomed. The main entrance was a cul-de-sac on the side of the building. Jack parked in the visitor lot and went in. The receptionist was in her early thirties. She was well groomed and very attractive. The name plate said Grace. "Good Morning, Sir, how can I help you?"

Jack thought for a split second. He carried his CID identification card out of habit. He thought some legerdemain was in order. "Yes, I need to see Mr. Wasserstein. Official business. He flashed the ID card hoping she was too naive to challenge it. She was startled for a moment, replied with, "Of course. One moment please." She picked up the phone and pressed a few buttons. After a few hushed words, she hung up and said "He will see you in a moment." It was around 11:15am and Jack looked around the lobby. Several pictures of Wasserstein and various local and state level celebrities. Even a few movie stars. No family pictures. He was looking at a picture of Wasserstein and a woman with her face obscured. There was something familiar about her but he couldn't place it. He was putting the picture down when a man about 6 feet tall came through the large ebony doors on the left side of the receptionist's desk. He was about 60 years old, distinguished gray temples and a ruddy complexion. He obviously spent a lot of time either in Florida or tanning or both. He was trim, jovial and confident. "Good Morning, Detective. How can I help you?"

"I need to speak with you. Privately, please."

"Of course. We can use my office." Jack followed Wasserstein into the large office. It took up a significant portion of the south side of the building. It was set up almost like a small apartment but with a large ebony desk towards the back. There was another room with ebony doors towards the back of the office to the right of the desk. Jack sensed someone was in that room but he turned his attention to the task at hand. "Mr. Wasserstein, I'm sure you're aware of the kidnapping in Langston?" Wasserstein's joviality disappeared. "Yes, I am aware of the incident."

"They've arrested a young man who is believed to be an accessory to the crime."

"Oh, really?" His response was very insincere, almost sarcastic. "Is there proof?"

That was an unusual response for someone being questioned about a crime they had nothing to do with. "No. Someone is pressing charges against Ethan Wass. I need to ask you some questions and I'm afraid that they may make you somewhat uncomfortable."

"I have a thick skin, Detective."

"Do you know Ethan Wass?"

"No."

"Do you know Maribeth Hanney?"

"No."

"Can you tell me anything about Mark Wass?

"I don't know anyone by that name."

"Mr. Wasserstein, I'm trying to save the lives of three young boys and possibly the life of Mark Wass. Now please, do you have any relationship with any of the people I mentioned?"

"Detective, I am not in the habit of answering useless inquiries. I'm sure you already know the answer to these questions."

"Mr. Wasserstein, I need you to confirm this 'theoretical' information I have. The only thing that matters is the lives of these kids."

"Alright, alright. Yes, I did know Maribeth Hanney and yes, I am aware that the boys are my grandsons. Unfortunately, I have had no contact with them since they were born. I fulfilled the agreement Maribeth and I had when she left."

"According to her she was fired."

"I had to. I couldn't run a business with a lot of loose ends."

Jack got a little indignant. "These are hardly loose ends! They are human beings! Children!"

"Detective, I was under the impression that she was on birth control. If she was untruthful about that, then it's not my fault."

"Regardless, they are your offspring. Did you make any provision for them in your will?"

"No. Legally I have no responsibility to them." Jack thought to make a moral plea but decided it would be fruitless. "Did you know the Christensens?"

"I did not."

"Is there anything else you can tell me? Anything about the boys or some known associates that might see them as a way to get to you?"

"I don't know what Maribeth has told you or anyone else. As far as I know there could be hundreds of men out there, trying to use those boys to get to me. Being successful in business means you make enemies. I have my share."

"Has anyone contacted you about a ransom for the boys?"

"No. I would pay it of course if it would guarantee their safety. Is that all?"

"I can't think of anything else, right now but I may have some additional questions later. I will be in touch." Jack turned to leave. Wasserstein followed him halfway to the door.

"I'm not a monster, Detective. I want to see those boys rescued as much as you do."

"Then I'm sure you will be willing to help in anyway, right?"

"Absolutely."

"I'll be in touch." Jack walked out at a brisk pace. Wasserstein lingered until he was gone. A figure emerged from the other room. "You are a cagey guy, Ben." Laurie Clark was standing by the door.

"I know Sis. Mr. Chase is very concerned about those boys."

"Well he's a teacher. A child lover at heart."

"Hmm. A pedophile. He shouldn't be working in schools."

"That's not funny. He is going to blow this thing wide open if we let him run around."

"You are the Superintendent. Doesn't he work for you?"

"Yes, but I'm on shaky ground with this indictment. If I shake things up too much, especially with Chase, he is going to catch on. He's pretty smart, and an experienced investigator from what I hear."

"Okay. We'll need to take care of him."

"How?"

"I know some specialists that can handle this problem. It seems that attacks on schools are popular these days."

"Oh, no no no no. No way. I can't afford to let anybody else get hurt. We are in this thing deep and we are going to have to be solid if we are going to get out of it.

"Suit yourself, dear sister. But there may come a time when you can't avoid the unsavory aspects of your current situation. I've been able to protect you thus far but my resources are dwindling fast. The warrant for Ethan, the elimination of the Christensen's, we either shut Mr. Chase down now or we may not get another chance."

"Let me think about it. The last thing this town needs is a school shooting." Clark was worried.

"As long as we have a specific target, it shouldn't be a problem. They go in the office, pick off Chase, wound a few others and it looks like a vendetta against an overly stern Vice Principal. Thanks to you, I have someone who can be that disgruntled student."

"The children, though-"

"Laurie, you lost your concern for the children the minute you embezzled that money from the school district. It was not easy to hide that fact. Right now, the only thing you need to focus on is self-preservation."

"All right, all right. Just Chase, no one else."

"I'll make the call."

Jack stopped in on Officer Riggs at the police station. He hoped that he had some useful information for him since his meeting with Wasserstein was rather dry. "Hey Jerry. Any news?"

Riggs turned around in his chair. "I had to pull a lot of favors."

"I appreciate it, Jerry. What did you come up with?

"I went through the court requests and tried to find the judge who signed the warrant. A judge named Charles Reubens. But the weird thing is that he didn't request it and didn't come from here. We don't know where or who requested it. This is odd because all that information should have been put into the computer by the court clerk who handled it."

"Do we know who the clerk is?"

"Not by name but by number. This was initiated by Clerk 76."

"What about Reubens?"

"Well no one knows too much about him. He came up from Pennsylvania about three years ago. Pittsburgh, from what I can tell. A Harvard grad, already licensed in Massachusetts but not he's not from here. A lot of this is from the internet. He had a law firm down there and it seemed to be doing well until about five years ago. Had a high-profile case that looked open and shut. They were a shoo in to win it until the prosecution brought in a surprise witness that blew the whole thing wide open. Politicians, wealthy businessmen, executives all caught in a sex for hire scandal."

"Yes, I remember that-the Briarwood Scandal. It was pretty bad."

"Anyway, Reubens was planning to run for state senator. Once his firm lost that case, all hell broke loose. He was almost disbarred for mishandling evidence. Somehow, he side-stepped that and all he got was a letter of censure. He could still practice law but his political career was finished before it started. The firm he worked for shut down fast and he left the state. He was on a sabbatical for about 4 months and then he showed up here. He was a junior defense lawyer for less than a year and then all of a sudden he's a judge."

"Sounds like he had some help moving up the ladder. Just for kicks and giggles, did he have any high-profile clients?"

"Just one of note. Benjamin Wasserstein."

"I figured as much. I have a feeling Mr. Wasserstein took a vested interest in a minor league defense lawyer so he'd eventually have a judge in his pocket. Good work, Jerry. You really came through."

"Like you said, I wouldn't be here if it weren't for you. All things considered, I hope you can help the Wass kid."

"Thanks. I've got some ammunition now, so maybe I can get somewhere with it. I'll let you know." Jack left the station and stopped by the school to update Scarley. He went to his office to plan his next move. Alma poked her head in the door. "Dinner tonight?"

"Sure. My place or yours?"

"My place about 7pm. I'm making lasagna."

"Love it. No onions or peppers, though-I'm allergic."

"What about garlic?"

"Garlic is fine. Sounds tasty."

"Ok, see you then."

Jack hadn't had lasagna in a long time. He used to make it for his wife and Dad when he was over. He turned back to his computer. He looked up Charles Reubens and confirmed a good amount of the information Jerry had given him. He lived in Concord, so Jack decided to give him a visit. It was unusual for a judge to live in a different county than they work. Concord was in Middlesex county but he was a Worcester County circuit judge. He was old school since his address and land line number were published. Jack left for Concord. It was a half hour drive so he had time to think. He suspected that Reubens was in Wasserstein's pocket. It still did not explain why Wasserstein would want to frame Ethan? Why would he kidnap the Hanney boys and kill the Christensens? Still no answers to the important questions. He figured he'd be straightforward with Reubens. He found the road and went down about half way. The house was a typical Concord mansion. The grounds were immaculate and the house was a beautiful colonial style, only about 5 years old. Jack drove up to the three-car garage and parked. He walked up to the front door and found it open. Jack pushed it open and heard a groaning sound. He called out Reubens's name and heard, "Here!" He followed the sound to the kitchen. On the floor in a pool of blood was a man struggling to move and holding his abdomen. "Judge Reubens?" Jack asked as he looked for something to stop the bleeding. The man nodded and tried to speak. "Please...listen to me…"

"Don't speak. Save your energy."

"No-I don't have much time. The warrant, phony. Those boys are alive."

"The boys? The Hanney boys?"

"Yes. Wasserstein. Tried to have me killed. I know everything. I.."

"Did he pay you to issue that warrant?"

"Yes. Blackmailed me too…" Reubens started to fade.

"Hold on. I'm calling 911."

"You must save those boys. Get to the ranges. South Post. Devens."

"How is Wasserstein blackmailing you?

"His lovers, not all female. He doesn't want anyone to know."

"How does that affect you?"

"I was one of them." Reubens was fading in and out. "My wife and kids don't know."

"Do you have any proof?"

"My computer, the app, Lockdown. I have it all there. Please don't tell my family. Please, don't-"

Reubens let out a breath and passed out. The paramedics came and called out into the foyer. Jack yelled, "In here!" They ran to Reubens and checked him. He was dead. Jack held back and looked for Reuben's computer. The state police showed up and cordoned off the area as a crime scene. Jack found the computer and was able to get a glance of the screen. It was a letter that Reubens was writing to confess and completely come clean about everything. The only thing missing was the affair he had with Wasserstein. Jack was an old-fashioned conservative but he strove to stay non-judgmental of people who were in the homosexual lifestyle. Really the only issue he had with Reubens is that he was cheating on his wife. "This must be why he was killed," Jack mused. He saw Reubens's cell phone and palmed it. He went down the hall when he heard someone calling out. "Hello? Anyone else here?"

Jack figured he'd better make himself known. He moved down towards the bathroom and went in. "Yes, I am here." A trooper came to the bathroom door. "Who are you?"

"My name is Jack Chase. I discovered the judge and called 911."

"What are you doing up here?", the trooper was female, about thirty years old. A sergeant.

"Can't stand the sight of blood. Plus, I tried to help him. Got it all over me." Jack exaggerated a little to avoid unnecessary questions.

"He was alive when you got here?" She seemed to relax her demeanor somewhat.

"Yes."

"Did he say who did this to him?"

"No. He was trying though."

"Why did you come to see him?"

Jack thought quickly. "Well he was referred to me as someone who interested in being a consultant for the young lawyer's club at my school. I'm a vice principal at Langston High School.

"Langston? That's kind of far isn't it?"

"Well, that's how the districts are set. Been that way for years."

"Okay, we'll need to check out your story."

"By all means. Here is my card, if you need to call me."

"All right, Mr. Chase. We'll be in touch."

Jack was relieved that he wasn't arrested. He got back to his car and drove straight home. It was about 6:30. He remembered that he was meeting Alma for dinner so he showered up and went over. He had Reubens's cell phone. He pondered whether or not he should go through with it. He told Alma what happened and she was horrified.

"So, he died in your arms?"

"Yeah, it was sad. I don't think he meant any harm. Still, Wasserstein had him by the shorthairs. He had written that confession but it doesn't make sense. He and Wasserstein were gay lovers, I can see how it would hurt them both, but why would Reubens come clean now? Before he died, he begged me not to tell his family."

"He was badly wounded. He could have been confused."

"I suppose. But it seemed an act of desperation. There was no break in. Whoever killed him either knew him, or had access to his house."

"Do you think Wasserstein had him killed?"

"Probably, the problem is how do we prove it? Also, we still don't know how the Hanney boys factor into things. We know that they are Wasserstein's sons, but he wants nothing to do with them." Jack's phone rings. "Hello? Hey Brian. What? When? Okay,l that's good news, I guess. Puzzling though. Ok. Yeah, see you in the morning." He hung up the phone.

Alma moved closer. "That was Brian. Ethan Wass has been released from prison."

"That's great!" Alma looked at Jack and he didn't seem happy about it. "Isn't it?" Jack took a long time to answer. "Yeah, it's great news. Awfully, darned convenient."

"What do you mean?"

"With Reubens out of the picture, Wasserstein has nobody in court that can do his bidding. Without him, I think the case against Ethan will fall apart."

"We didn't want Ethan in trouble anyway, right?"

"True. But maybe he's in a different kind of trouble. They killed Reubens. They could just as easily take out Ethan or even the Hanney boys."

"Do you think Ethan is in danger?"

"Yes, I do and if we don't do something, he and the Hanneys will be in grave danger, too!"

It was quarter of eight at night. The phone rang at the station. "Is Officer Riggs there?"

"Yes, just a moment." The phone went silent for about half a minute. "This is Riggs."

"Jerry! Jack Chase, here. Listen Ethan Wass has been released and the charges dropped."

"Yeah I just heard. That's good news."

"I believe he is in danger. Can you get to him?"

"They were keeping him at Devens. His mother is supposed to be picking him up."

"How fast can you get there?"

"About 15 minutes."

"Make it ten. I think I know where they're going to take him out."

Riggs jumped into a squad car and sped off. Jack threw on some sweatpants and a hoodie and started to leave. "Alma this could get hairy. Would you stay here for me, please? Don't open the door for anyone except me."

"Sure, Sweetums." She planted a kiss right on Jack's lips. "You're sexy when you're playing hero. Go get 'em." Jack smiled and left. He heard the reassuring sound of a door locking so he knew Alma would be safe.

Jack went as fast as he could and met Jerry at the entrance to the holding facility. Devens was medium security so the pulled right up to the gate. Everything was quiet and a car pulled up behind them. Martha Wass got out and walked over to them.

"What's going here? Why are you guys here?"

Jack spoke up, "We believe that Ethan's life is in danger. We came to make sure he was ok."

"Why do you think that? They dropped the charges against him and I've come to take him home."

"It's a long story, Martha. We just need to make sure. Hopefully, we're wrong."

A noise behind them made Jack turn around quickly. It was the first gate opening and a guard and Ethan walked through. They made it to the final gate when a loud, scattered, pinging sound erupt out of the night air. Bullets sprayed all over the fenced gate area where Ethan was. Jack grabbed Martha and dove behind the squad car while the guard was hit multiple times. Jerry took cover and Ethan hit the ground as well. The guard, wounded but alive shielded Ethan. Jerry drew his gun and fired back towards the direction of the shots. A large black van roared and bolted from the dark and blasted down the driveway. Jerry continued shooting until the van was out of range. He had shot through the passenger side window and saw a figure, flailing. Jack ran over to Ethan. He had been hit but not seriously. Martha ran over too. "Ethan!" She cried. "Ethan are you okay?"

"Yes, Mom. I'll live." Martha cradled him and cried a little. Jerry call for an ambulance. The guard had taken most of the shots. He was alive but barely. Two ambulances had come and tended to the wounded. They stabilized the guard and loaded him into one of the ambulances. Two other cruisers had shown up. One was Jerry's superior officer Captain LeBlanc and the Prison Watch Commander., LT Farley. "Riggs! What the hell is going on?"

Jack spoke up. "Captain, I can explain."

"Mr. Chase? What are you doing here?"

"In a nutshell, we believe that Ethan's life was in danger. I asked Officer Riggs to help make sure Ethan was okay." From there Jack told LeBlanc about the whole thing. "You don't have any proof, yet?"

"Not yet. Right now, I was just concerned about Ethan. Without Judge Reubens, he won't be charged."

"Okay. I will look into this personally. For now, Mr. Chase please go home and leave the detective work to us. Riggs, I want all the information you have on this, on my desk, first thing in the morning."

"Yes, Sir!" Riggs seemed pleased with himself. "I was trying to make detective. if this goes right, I may just get it."

Jack started to relax. "You might, Jerry, you just might."

Alma was waiting for Jack when he got home. It was almost midnight. "Are you okay?"

"Yes, Alma. I was right. They tried to kill Ethan tonight. They were professionals. They seemed more interested in getting away than getting him though. Still it's in the police's hands now. Captain LeBlanc is aware of the caper and he's taking over."

"Oh, Thank God. I was getting scared we were in too deep. I don't want Wasserstein coming after us."

"I wouldn't worry. I don't think he can afford to."

The next morning, Jack left for school early to catch up on some work. Alma had to drop her car off for service so she took the morning off. Jack was in his office when he heard a strange sound. He looked outside the office in the hall and didn't see anything unusual. He had an uneasy feeling but shrugged it off. A large van pulled up in front of the school. There was signage on the side, "Boore Telephone Services". Jack assumed they were here to finally fix the phone lines and the intercom system. He thought that since the intercom system was ancient and since the new school would have everything updated, they would continue to piecemeal and jerry-rigg this one until they moved. Jack chuckled at the term 'jerry rigg'. He decided to go to the teacher's lounge for coffee since Alma wasn't around to make it in the office. He never could get the Keurig machine to work right. He secured a cup and started to return to the office when he heard some crashing sound followed by shooting. Dozens of students came out of the classrooms along with teachers to see what the noise was. Three masked men came out of the office. Jack dropped his coffee and screamed, "Everyone back in the room! Bar the doors!!!" One of the masked men looked over and saw Jack. He raised his weapon to shoot when a teacher broadsided him. The gunman rolled over and the teacher wrestled him for it. The gun went off and the teacher was underneath the gunman. Jack ran to them and called out, "Bobby! Bobby!" The teacher pushed the gun man off of him and said, "I'm okay!" Jack looked up and saw the office had been showered with bullets. He went in to see if anyone was hurt. He saw Scarley in his desk chair. Dead from multiple gun shots. Jack wept for his friend for a moment. He went back to the dead gunman and removed his mask. It wasn't anyone he recognized so he went after the other two.

The old building had a few secrets. Jack liked that about the school so he used them to his advantage. He dialed 911 as left the office. He knew that students could be hurt so he had to neutralize the threat immediately. He heard more shooting in the English wing. He ran over and peered down the hall. Debris was falling from the ceiling so Jack assumed the gunman shot up in the air. His voice was gravelly and mean.

"Where's the vice principal?" He ordered.

"We don't know! I haven't seen him!" Mrs. Lizotte, a World Lit teacher cried. "He would be in the office if he were here."

"Find him! Or I will start picking off teenagers!"

Mrs. Lizotte screamed, "Nooooooo" and moved towards the gunman. He slapped her hard and then pointed the automatic weapon at her head. Jack screamed, "Wait!!! I'm the one you want!!" The gunman looked up and started back down the hallway. Jack dashed off towards the History wing, past the office. He ducked into the Yearbook office and found an old, blocked off hallway that led into the courtyard. He set the board that covered the door aside and looked out into the hallway. The gunman was moving fast so Jack ducked into the old hallway, pulled the board up to the door and set it in place. He waited a moment while the confused gunman looked in the room. He called Jack's name and looked around. He went into the hall and continued towards the foreign language wing. Jack cut through the Courtyard and waited outside the door to went back into the hallway into the Foreign Language wing. He saw the gunman through the window and waited until he came up to the door. Jack blasted through the door and knocked the gunman to the floor. He punched the gunman and wrestled him for the gun. Jack grabbed the gun and knocked out the gunman with the butt of the weapon. He dragged him into the courtyard and barred the door. He then looked around for the other gunman. It was eerily quiet as Jack moved from the Foreign Language wing to the math department. He checked the rooms and most of the students huddled in the corner. He instructed them to get out of the building, but be very quiet. He went down the stairs into the cafeteria and he heard shouting coming from the gym hallway. He rushed up to the first gym door and stopped. He stared in horror as he saw the third gunman hold a student by the neck at gunpoint. He moved slowly towards them. "That's far enough!" The masked gunman seemed fairly young. "One more step and I'll blow his head off!"

"Listen to me. This isn't going to end well for you. If you let him go, we can end this peacefully."

"That ship has sailed. I'm walking out of here. Now."

"Then take me and leave him." The students gasped. It was like a bad movie where the hero is sacrificing himself for the sake of the innocent bystanders. "Okay, you come and take his place." Jack put down his weapon and walked towards the gunman. The student moved away but stared at Jack. "It'll be okay." Jack reassured him. "Let's go." Jack and the gunman walked out into the hall. The outside door was about 6 yards down. Jack knew he had only a few moments to decide his next move. He decided to get the gunman out of the school. He figured the outside doors were locked and the gunman wouldn't be able to get back in. "Open the door."

Jack obeyed him and as they came to the stairs, the gunman tripped. Out of instinct, Jack broke free and cold-cocked him. He ran off towards the new school to draw him away from the students. "Chase!!" The gunman seemed to know him. He ran into an opening and tried to lose him. The gunman ran in. Jack ran up the stairs. "You can't escape, Chase. This was for you!!"

"What do you mean, 'for me'?"

"This was all for you. To die. To be the victim of another school shooting!"

Jack was horrified. Scarley was murdered because he was in the wrong place at the wrong time. He went from horror to rage. His friend was dead because someone wanted him out of the way. The sheer brutality and disregard for life infuriated him. "You seem to know me. Who are you?"

"Shut Up! You don't get to ask questions. It's your fault I have no future! Now I'm taking yours!" The gunman pulled out a pistol and fired in Jack's direction. He moved down an unfinished hallway. The gunman followed him. Jack had to get him talking. "You were one of my students?"

"You could call it that. You kicked me out."

"Why?"

"Because you're a jerk!" He fired towards the sound. "I joined the Army. I did two years."

"Congratulations. It's sounds like you had a future after all!" "Wrong! I tried to become an officer, but I had to go to college. Because of you expelling me, no decent college would take me!"

"There's nothing wrong with being an enlisted man. That's how I started."

"The Army wouldn't let me reenlist after I got into a fight with my Lieutenant. They cut me a deal-some deal!"

"Let me guess. They gave you a choice of doing time or getting out, right?"

"I wasn't going to jail! They kicked me out and barred me from the service. No future!!" He shot some more. Jack had an idea of who the gunman was. "You could have come to talk to me. Even after expulsion I would have helped you."

"No, you wouldn't have! You don't care about me! You just care about those goody two shoes like Ethan Wass and those Hanney brats!" Jack was trying to get a bead on the gunman and stumbled. He fell through a hole in the unfinished floor and fell right behind him. The gunman spun around and Jack grabbed the gun. The gunman threw a punch and missed. Jack grabbed his arm and spun him around. The gunman broke away and threw another punch. Jack deflected it and used his arm against him. He pinned him to the wall and held him. "Listen to me! Scarley is dead-that makes you an accessory to murder. Unless you let me help you, you are going to go to jail."

"You had your chance. You could've helped me years ago!" The gunman broke free and shoved Jack away. Jack grabbed for him and caught his mask and pulled it off. It was Will Turner. Jack figured it was him. Turner reached down for Jack's throat, but again Jack was able to deflect him and kicked him in the stomach. It took the wind out of him and he fell back onto the floor. Jack got up and went over to Turner. "Will, I can't change the past, but if you help me, I may be able to help you now. Who ordered the hit on me?

Turner was having trouble breathing. "Ben Wasserstein."

"Why?"

"He said you were getting too close to the truth. He wanted you out of the way. You were the only one to be killed but the guys I was with didn't care who got hurt. They went into the office and thought Scarley was you. When they realized they killed the wrong guy they had to make it look like a random school shooting." Turner was wheezing and coughing.
"Does Wasserstein have anything to do with the Hanney boys' kidnapping?"

"He has them holed up at his office on Devens. He's got Clark there, too."

"Clark? He kidnapped her?

"No, she comes and goes as she pleases. He calls her, "Sis." Will was having a lot of trouble speaking and breathing. Jack looked down and saw a piece of metal sticking out of Will's side. "You're hurt. I gotta call an ambulance."

"Listen, if I do one thing right it'll be this. Those other guys, with me on this, are the same guys that took those boys and killed those old people. Wasserstein has another place and he has a guy who he has kept there. All the proof you need is in his office. I have hidden a recorder and a thumb drive with the same information on it. Insurance, I guess. Fat lot of good it did me." Turner faded and passed out. Jack checked his pulse and he was still alive. The metal rod that pierced him was the only thing keeping the blood from running everywhere. Fortunately, the paramedics found him were able to stabilize Turner. Jack went back to the school and the state police SWAT Team was debriefing everyone. Several of the student's' parents had come to take their kids home. Jack saw a single body bag in the office. He was starting to tear up a little until he heard a voice. Laurie Clark was there and speaking to the SWAT captain. Jack was incensed when he saw her but played it cool. He went over to her. He decided that he would try to pump her for information. "Laurie, I…" She interrupted him, "Oh Jack, I am so sorry about Brian. I know you two were friends." Jack was really struggling to keep his composure. "Thanks. What do we know about the attackers?"

"Not much," The SWAT captain broke in. "Most you already know. Three men, one dead. The other two in custody."

"The injured one is a former student. Will Turner." Jack said.

"Did he say anything?" Clark asked quickly. "No, he was unconscious. I tried to stop the bleeding but he needed more help."

"Oh, that's good." Clark seemed only slightly relieved when Jack made her believe Will hasn't said anything. He figured that because of this botched assassination attempt, Turner's life could be in danger. He figured Wasserstein would bump him off to keep him from talking. Jack had an idea. He pulled the SWAT captain aside. "I need you to do me a favor."

"I'll try."

"Some people may take revenge against the Turner kid. Can we get him some protection at the hospital?"

"Sure, I think under the circumstances, we can arrange that."

"Thanks."

Jack checked the school for any lingering students and then left. He went out to his car and called Captain LeBlanc. "We don't have much time."

Turner had been in surgery at Heywood Memorial Hospital for almost 8 hours. Once he was stable, he was moved to intensive care. A figure in scrubs and a face mask showed up about midnight and headed towards Turner's room. Once inside the room, the figure took out a syringe and injected the contents into the I.V. drip port. The room was dark except a small light next to the bed. Turner was on his side and covered with a blanket so his face was obscured. As the figure injected the poison into the port, she whispered, "I'm so sorry". All of a sudden, the full room lights flashed on. The person at the light switch was Captain LeBlanc. "Stop right there. You are under arrest for murder one, attempted murder, and embezzlement."

The figure was shocked. "Th..th.. this isn't what it looks like!"

"It looks like you are trying to silence Will Turner!" The person in the bed flung the cover off. It was not Turner, but Jack Chase. "You were trying to cover your tracks, like you've been doing for several years, haven't you, Laurie!"

"What? No, I didn't..." Jack pulled the mask off of the figure and it was Laurie Clark.

"You embezzled the money from the school district and asked your wealthy brother to help you cover it up. He had his own secrets that were about to come out. You concocted a desperate plan to fake a kidnapping and pin it on a former student. When that wasn't working and I was asking too many questions, you found another former student with an axe to grind. You had him and two others who were hired thugs, storm the school with the intention of shutting me up. I imagine those two were probably the same idiots who kidnapped the Hanney boys and killed their grandparents."

"I don't know anything about that!"

"Will suspected he might need some insurance in case things went south." Jack pulled out a small digital recorder. This was hidden in Wasserstein's office. It's a voice activated recorder, and it has all the evidence we need to gather a conviction against you and your brother. Right now, there is a rescue team with a warrant heading to Ben's office on Devens. I'm sure we will find the Hanney boys holed up in there."

"That recording is inadmissible as evidence! You won't be able convict me on embezzlement!" Clark was panicking.

"Maybe not, that's up to the judge. But we have two witnesses here, now that saw you inject that stuff into the I.V. All we need to do is have it analyzed and we can bust you for attempted murder."

"You have the right to remain silent." Captain LeBlanc pulled out hand-cuffs and took Clark into custody. "You haven't heard the last of me!"

"Didn't you hear the Captain? You have the right to remain silent, I suggest you do so." Jack said, moving close to her face. Clark grimaced as the captain put the cuffs on and led her out to a police car. Jack turned around and opened a curtain that concealed the other bed. Will Turner was weak, but alive. "Mr. Chase, Thank you."

"My pleasure Will. Without your cooperation, we wouldn't have been able to get Clark. Now we have to take down Wasserstein. You're safe now. Rest easy."

Jack was glad to have helped Turner. Clark was on her way to jail and this was something she could not weasel out of. They would reinstate the first indictment which will take care of the money she stole and the attempted murder and kidnapping charges. Plus, the Christensen's deaths should put Laurie Clark away for a long time. Wasserstein was in as deep as Laurie. Jack was heading home when he got a call from Officer Jerry Riggs.

"Captain wanted me to tell you. They got to Wasserstein's office and they didn't find the boys."

"Damn. Any leads?"

"Not yet. The computers were wiped and he emptied his safe."

"Okay. So, he's on the run and has the boys with him. We need to find him. Did they check his security cameras?"

"They're working on that now. I'll let you know when they are done."

"Thanks, Jerry."

Jack hung up the phone. He had forgotten how late it was. He hadn't eaten and it was already after 1am. He knew the McDonald's at the rotary in Nashoba was open 24 hours so he grabbed a chicken sandwich and went over to Wasserstein's office. He met Riggs and several other officers combing through Wasserstein's building. "Anything from the cameras?" He asked Riggs.

"Yeah we just got it in. Fortunately, he was too arrogant to secure the footage." They sat down and Grace, the young receptionist, opened up the program. She obviously did not expect to come in at such a late hour. "This is today." She clicked the play button. "Just make sure you put him away. He's hit on every female in this building just about. He placed the Human Resources department in Boston, just so they couldn't bother him. Plus, if he has those boys, I want him to suffer."

"I'll see what I can do." Jack and Riggs watched the footage. The room was empty. There were only cameras in the main office, none in the side room. "What was in that other room?"

"We dubbed it, 'The Pleasure Palace.' Anytime Wasserstein was 'entertaining' someone he took them in there. I suppose it's harmless enough but since he was such a womanizer...."

"Not just women." Jack paused for effect. Grace was initially surprised, but then realized it made sense. "This man came often," She pointed to a ragged figure coming in. It appeared that the ragged man and Wasserstein had a heated argument. They stopped when two small figures came in from the Pleasure Palace. The ragged man went over and hugged the two boys, said something to Wasserstein and then left. "Grace, who is this guy?"

"I'm not sure but he came about every other day."

"Those two have to be the Hanney boys." Jack was relieved that they were unharmed.

"Can you go back a few days? Around three weeks ago?"

"Sure, we keep a year's worth of footage for insurance purposes. I had the system set up. I tweaked it, in case he got out of hand."

"Wow, gorgeous and brilliant." Riggs was taking a liking to her. She went back to the day of the kidnapping. About an hour after the kidnapping, they witnessed several people enter the office. There was Wasserstein, Clark, two thuggish looking men with sacks over their shoulders and the ragged man from the previous day. The ragged man was extremely upset.

"Is there any sound?" Jack was hoping that Grace, put that into the system. "Yes, but the microphone was only in one place. I place several books on a shelf for decoration and put a mic there, again for some kind protection. If he said anything off color, I would at least have that. I wanted to have a lot of audio should I ever get on the wrong side of him. He wasn't horrible to work for, most of the time. It was pretty much, business as usual, but after he closed a big contract, he would get frisky. And inappropriate. So, I put a Bible as one of the books to cover the mic. I figured he'd never read it and I told him people would trust him more if he had it there.

"Clever lady. So, what do we have?"

"Let me turn it up."

She brought up the volume and pressed play:

Ragged Man: You are unbelievable! You'd use your own grandsons to control me?

Ben: Look, you know I will do whatever I can to protect my interests. I am going to leave them my fortune. It's not much to ask.

Ragged Man: YOUR IDIOT HENCHMEN KILLED THE OTHER GRANDPARENTS! ARE YOU OUT OF YOUR MIND?

Ben: That was unfortunate. But they would have been able to derail this entire plan. Also, they know who you are!

Ragged Man: Those idiots killed them in front of the boys! You've scarred them like you've scarred me!

Ben: The Christensens were collateral damage.

Ragged Man: Is every person a pawn in your grand scheme? I cannot believe I was born from such an evil man.

Ben: Oh, come off your high horse! You don't get to lecture me about morality! You've taken the money I gave you!

Ragged Man: You never really gave me a choice, did you? You black-mailed me to leave my family and then you pay me? That's just sick. I figured at least my wife and son could have comfortable life if I couldn't be with them. And then because you were pissed at me, you set up my son, your other grandson. You really are a sick bastard.

Ben: I've built my business this way and-

Ragged Man: Sacrificed your family in return! I would have gladly given up all the trappings and houses and private schools and all of it to have a loving father and mother. A normal family life. Instead your greed has made you a monster! You can spend your life salving your conscience with money but I was determined to be the father I never had.

Ben: Cry me a river, Mark. You took the money and now you are part of this just the same. Those boys won't be hurt but I need them right now.

Ragged Man: You listen to me. I am going to come here every day and check on those boys. If their father won't care about them, their older half-brother will.

"Wow. This is like a bad soap opera." Jack still needed more information. "Grace, can you download all the footage from this? We'll need to go through all of it."

"Sure, I'll use an external hard drive and get it to you in the morning."

"Great. School is closed until further notice so I will go through it at home. Jerry, I will give you a call when I am done."

"I have tomorrow off so why don't I stop by midafternoon?"

"Okay. Sounds, good. Thanks, Grace." Jack walked out to his car and went home. It was around 3:30am.

Jack woke up with a start. His phone was ringing and he hadn't finished sleeping. "Hello?"

"Mr. Chase, this is Ben Wasserstein."

"What do you want?"

"I think you know."

"Actually, I don't. You'll forgive me I was up pretty late last night."

"I'll make this simple. Give me the security tape footage along with all the evidence against me and Laurie Clark."

"Now why would I do that? Plus, what makes you think I have it?"

"You either have it or you know who does. I don't have a great deal of time, Mr. Chase. The evidence in one hour, else you'll never see those boys again."

"Good Lord, Man! Those are your sons! Why on earth would you want to harm them?"

"You've been more of a father to them than I have, Chase. One hour. No police." The call went dead. Jack had to figure out a way to free those boys without letting Wasserstein off the hook. He called Riggs. "We have a problem. Wasserstein just called me wanting to trade the Hanney boys for all the evidence on him and Clark. I know it's early but did you find anything on the tapes?"

"No, I just woke up."

"He's given me an hour and no police."

"Alright, let me see what I can do. Give me twenty minutes."

"Okay, call me."

Jack sat up on the bed. He thought an hour had passed when the phone rang again. It was Riggs number but Grace spoke. "I think I can save you some time. I can access company records from my house and I think I know what Wasserstein wants."

"Great but why are you on Riggs phone?"

"He's right here. Anyway, come over here so I can show you. I live at 32 Riverside Lane, Forestville. Apartment 32508."

"On my way."

Jack threw on some sweats and rushed over to Grace's house. He buzzed in and went up to the third floor. He knocked on the door and it swung open. Riggs was standing next to Grace as she sat at the computer. "He's broke."

"What?" Jack said.

"On top of murder, kidnapping and conspiracy, eight years ago, he embezzled millions of dollars from his investors. It was easy for him-he'd secure large sums from investors and forged documents showing profits, mergers, and even going public. He was on borrowed time." Riggs reported.

"So, he was hemorrhaging cash."

Grace began to explain. "Yes, but about three years ago, he had a huge influx of cash which just about covered his shortcomings. About $17 million."

"That's about when the $20 million from the school district went missing. I will bet that Clark gave most of it to Wasserstein."

"That would make sense. They must have helped each other. He wrote several large checks to the Langston school district over the last two years."

Jack thought for a moment. "He was subsidizing the district to cover the $20 million. Every time the budget came up short, Clark said she could cover it with funds from some wealthy benefactor that she never named. Once she said she'd cover it herself, claiming it was her inheritance from her father. She was using the money she stole to help her brother and he was paying her back."

"Embezzlement and bad money management runs in the family, apparently." Grace was pleased that she was able to put the caper together. "What now?"

"We make Wasserstein think that he will get what he wants. First though we need to send this information to the authorities. I know somebody at the FBI I can send it to. We worked together on some joint operations." Jack took out his cell and left the room to call his friend. After a few minutes he came back. "All set. Here's the e-mail to send it to. Make a couple of copies to be safe." Jack looked at the clock and saw that it was 9:45. "I have to call him." He walked back into the other room. "Wasserstein, it's Chase."

"Okay you are to meet us at a neutral place. Say the Whitney Mall Parking lot. Near the back, by the creek. Call me when you get there. Do not mess this up. I want that information."

"You'll get it. Make sure you have those boys with you." Jack was as stern as he had ever been.

"I am many things, Mr. Chase. But I am a man of my word."

"You'll forgive me if I don't believe you. The boys, unharmed." Jack hung up first to show dominance. He went back into the living room. "I'm heading out. Be prepared to follow us in case he gets cute. Use your own car, we don't want to spook him."

Riggs responded, "He doesn't know me so it should be easy. Where are you meeting him?"

"Whitney Mall parking lot. Back by the creek."

"Okay. Let's Roll."

Jack pulled into the lot and looked around. He didn't see anything so he waited. After five minutes, his cell rings. "Mr. Chase."

"Wasserstein, where the hell are you? You were supposed to bring the boys and do this."

"I realize that. I needed to know you weren't followed. Meet me over at Home Depot."

"If this is a trick, I'm calling the police."

"Do that and you'll never see the boys again. Home Depot."

"No more games, Wasserstein."

Jack drove down the road to Home Depot. He parked and his phone rang again.

"Okay Mr. Chase, come to the appliance section. I will be there."

"Alright." Jack hurried to the appliance section. There was a consultant's desk and a couple of chairs. The boys were in the chairs and Wasserstein was standing behind the desk. Jack approached carefully. "You boys okay?" They nodded but they were noticeably scared. "Let's get this over with."

"Yes, let's. The evidence."

Jack reached into his pocket and pulled out a thumb drive. "I hope there's more than that. All that footage can't possibly fit on that."

Jack looked him down. "It's in my car. I had to know the boys were safe. We will walk out, casually. The boys will get into my car and I will give you the external drive."

"Fine, no tricks. I have some insurance." Wasserstein opened his coat slightly, enough to show the sidearm he had on his hip. "Let's go."

The group walked out at a normal pace, but it felt like an eternity to Jack. They went to his car and he unlocked it with his fob. He instructed the boys to get in and close the door. Jack pressed his fob again to pop open the trunk. He reached in to grab a small, black bag. "Here." Wasserstein opened the bag to reveal a black box, shaped somewhat like a book. "The cord is in there, too."

"Very nice doing business with you. I'd end you but around here there are too many witnesses."

"Go to hell, Wasserstein."

"Probably. But at least I will go in style!" He smiled and turned to walk away. Jack got into the car and started it up. He hadn't put it into gear when one of the boys said, "Mr. Chase, he booby trapped us!"

"What do you mean?"

The older boy unzipped his shirt and there was a homemade bomb strapped to his chest. Jack quickly unzipped the younger boy's coat a found a similar device. Both seemed to have a remote sensor attached to it so someone with either a transmitter or even a cell phone would set them off. "That monster." Jack thought. But he had an idea. "Sit tight boys this is almost over!" He whipped the wheel around and drove over to Wasserstein getting into a car. He blocked it and got out. Jack was infuriated but he knew he did not have much time. "WASSERSTEIN!" Ben saw him and turned white. "Get out of the way!"

"You unbelievable bastard!! Deactivate the bombs! NOW!"

"Or what? You'll kill me? Only I can disarm them. You didn't think I was that naive, did you?"

Jack was incensed. "You used innocent children, you friggin terrorist!" He punched him and bloodied his nose then grabbed him by the shirt. Jack knew he had to keep him near the boys so he wouldn't set them off and kill himself in the process. Wasserstein tried for his gun but Jack began to pummel him. The gun fell on the ground and Jack shoved it away. After exchanging blows, Jack finally got the upper hand.

"Where's the detonator?"

"Piss off!" Wasserstein remained defiant. Jack delivered another blow to the stomach. "Where is it? I'm not asking again!"

"You're not going to kill me. You wouldn't risk those two brats! I know you're keeping me close to them so we all don't get blown to bits. Smart move by the way."

Jack punched him in the jaw again. He had him on the ground when he heard a young voice, "Mr. Chase! Mr. Chase! We are okay! We got them off! It was the Johnny the older Hanney boy. Chase let Wasserstein up. "You're going to jail, you sick son a bitch!"

"No chance," he wheezed. "Not while I have this." He held up a small box with a button.

"Don't be a fool, Wasserstein!"

"I'm going to go now. You will not stop me! You stay away!" Wasserstein backed away towards his car. He slid in while holding up the detonator. He hastily put the car in reverse and then drive to clear Jack's car. He sped down the road towards the highway. Once he blasted through the light at the intersection, he turned left onto the Connector. Jack was collecting himself when he heard a relatively loud explosion. He and the Hanney boys were startled by the noise. A thought came to Jack, as Riggs and the FBI approached them. Jack turned to Bobby. "Bobby, where did you put those bomb vests?"

Bobby smiled a cheeky smile and said, "The back seat of his car." Jack smiled and breathed a sigh of relief and hugged Bobby. Matthew, Johnny's youngest brother came over and asked, "Mr. Chase can we go home now?"

"Sure, kiddo. I'm sure your Mom is itching to see you."

Alma was waiting at the Hanney's house, and Maribeth Hanney was waiting anxiously to see her sons. Jack pulled up to the house and stopped. They jumped out of the car and she ran to them almost knocking Jack over. She cried and hugged her sons. When she finally composed herself, she hugged Jack. "Thank you!" She said through teary eyes. "My pleasure. I'm glad they are okay." Alma threw her arms around Jack and they kissed. "There's lasagna for you at home."

Jack smiled and put her in his car.

PART II.

Chase's Gambit

Jack and Alma were enjoying each other. They had been officially dating for about six months and things were going better than they had
hoped. The school community accepted them and they kept things professional while they were at school. The school year progressed well
after the Hanney kidnapping and much healing had occurred. Dis-
graced former school superintendent Laurie Clark was indicted on
charges federal embezzlement, fraud and accessory to murder. Corrupt
businessman Ben Wasserstein was recovering in the hospital after being blown up by his own explosives. He was indicted in his hospital
bed and when he's well enough he will be tried on murder, conspiracy

to commit murder, kidnapping, wiretapping and a host of other charges. Things were wrapping up nicely. Unfortunately, there was one casualty. Brian Scarley, the former principal. He was a good man and well-liked by the students and faculty. His death was an awful tragedy. The school board felt having a grief counselor available would be advantageous for everyone, teachers and staff as well as students. Jack had stepped in to the position as interim principal. He was glad to do it and felt he was honoring his friend. The school board hired an interim superintendent, Walter Sampson. He was introduced at a special school board meeting at the end of January. It was the first meeting since the events of last fall; the school board wanted the community to have the Christmas season unfettered by administrative repairs to the school.

The rest of the school year was uneventful. It's late April and everyone was preparing for finals. The seniors had started their exams, since they would be finished before the other grades. Prom and graduation preparations provided a nice distraction from the tragic events of last fall. Jack was helping some students prepare for the SAT. They met after school. He was in the library when Alma came in.

"Hey."

"Hey there."

"Do you have a minute?"

"Sure." They stepped into the library office. "What's up?"

"I'm concerned about a few students."

"Oh? Why?"

"They went to a retreat last weekend and they haven't come back."

"What kind of a retreat?"

"Some kind of church retreat. They went with some Pastor and they haven't come back. Their parents are waiting for you in your office."

"Hmm. Weird. I'll be right there."

"I'll move them to Conference room 1."

"Okay. Be there in five minutes."

"We are very scared, Mr. Chase."

"I understand. Please call me Jack. What can you tell me about the church?"

Mona Frost was worried. "It's very strange. It's called, 'The Freedom'. They do a lot of proselytizing online. They have their in-person services on Friday nights and other events on weekends."

"Where do they have them?"

"At the community center in Goodrichville."

"Have any of you been to a service?"

"No, that's the odd thing." Jim Braithwaite had twins who were involved. Like Jack, he was a single father. "It was weird. A few other parents knew this about guy but they didn't say much about him. When this 'retreat' came up, this Pastor Bill person wouldn't let any other adults go. I offered to be a chaperone, but he refused. I was going to stop my girls from going but their 'minister' paid me a visit."

"A visit?" Jack shifted in his chair.

"Yeah, this leader of theirs came to my house and the girls ran to him, like they used to run to me when they were little. Anyway, we sat down and talked for a while."

"About what?"

"He laid out this whole concept about how we need to teach and nurture our children through his philosophy and such. It sounded like a lot of new age mumbo-jumbo. None of it seemed too far out there, and the girls were excited to go. So, against my gut feeling, I let them. Now I wish I hadn't."

The group murmured the same sentiment. The hair stood up on the back of Jack's neck. "This minister visited all of you?" There was a collective affirmation. "What is this guy's name?"

Amy Hoffman spoke up. "They call him Pastor Bill."

"No last name?"

Amy shook her head. "No. I actually told Mark he couldn't go until I got more information about this guy and this church but he snuck out. It's so unlike him."

"He's been acting out since his father died. Nothing awful, just the occasional attitude issue."

Jack knew Mark. "I remember. I told him that I knew how he felt since my wife died. He seemed to respond to that."

"He told me. He said it was nice to talk to someone who understood."

Jack smiled for a moment. "Okay. So, none of you have seen your kids since Friday night?"

"Right."

"So, any of you filed a missing person's report with the police?" Everyone raised a hand. "And they haven't responded?"

Jim spoke. "They are investigating, but we have more confidence in you, Jack. You were CID, plus you saved the Hanney boys. We can't wait for police procedure. A few of us were talking about having you investigate and we'd even pay you."

Jack was apprehensive. "I appreciate the confidence but I am not a licensed investigator." The parents looked desperate and a few on the edge of tears. "But these are my students so I will dig around and see what I can find out."

Before everyone left, Jack collected as much information as he could-what the kids were wearing, recent pictures, and friends they had who were part of Pastor Bill's 'church'. He decided to go to the community center in Goodrichville. He pulled up to the door as an older woman was locking the door. "Excuse me, do you know where I can find Pastor Bill?"

The woman frowned at the mention of the name. "That guy? Hmmph. No, but if you find him before I do, tell him he owes me three month's rent."

"You haven't seen him recently?"

"Not for a week. He had his meeting with all those kids and then they left."

"Do you know where they went?"

"I overheard one of the kids saying they were headed to Lake Dennison State Park. I hope that rickety bus got them there."

"How long has Pastor Bill been renting the hall?" Jack was leaning against his car.

"Almost a year. He put down six month's rent in advance and said he was starting a church. He called it 'The Freedom' or something." The woman trailed off as if she remembered something. "What is it?" Jack asked.

"When he said that, he corrected himself and said he was moving his church. It was very odd."

Jack pondered. "I'm not sure this guy is a genuine minister. The kids he was with last weekend haven't come home." The woman gasped. Jack paused for a moment. "Is there anything else you can tell me about this man?"

"I can do more than that. Come with me." Jack followed the woman around the back of the building. "This is the private entrance. He is renting this back apartment. Since he paid three months in advance, I threw it in with the hall. He was living here." The woman unlocked the door and swung the door open. It was a simple studio apartment, but there were stacks of paper lying around, photographs of children of various ages and a lock box. "It looks like he left in a hurry." Jack shifted into full investigator mode. "Do you mind if I look around? I need to figure out what's going on."

"You go ahead, young man. My name is Lorna Brown. I live in the big farmhouse up the street. The town owns this property but they bought it from my late husband so I have a key to everything and the town has me caring for it. Here are the keys to the hall as well. When you're done just drop them in the mailbox at 68 Goodrich St."

"Thank you, Lorna. I'm Jack Chase."

"The vice principal that found the Hanney boys?"

"Yes, Ma'am."

Lorna sighed heavily. "Just find those kids. That's more important than my rent money."

Jack nodded at the noble statement. Lorna closed the door and Jack began a detailed examination of the room. He started with the photographs. He saw photos of children as young as five and as old as fifteen or sixteen. As he sifted through the photos, he became more alarmed. Many of the pictures were normal, some even nice portraits. But as Jack dug deeper, he found risqué material, most illegal and many looking like they were taken under duress. He moved some of the photos and found some "church" literature. It was colorful and offered a lot of things of teen interest. He also found bank statements that showed that Pastor Bill had more than enough money to pay his rent. They were cash deposits of anywhere from $1000 to over $100,000. "This is a lot of money for a minister." Jack thought. He continued to comb through the paperwork and he found a laminated ledger page and a map of Lake Dennison State Park. There were three red circles on it and grid coordinates on the map. The ledger page was numbered with six to eighteen in the left column and an ascending dollar amount corresponding on the right. Jack knew that anything he took from here would be not be admissible in court, due to it being an unlawful search. He felt that the kids were in danger, so he took the map, snapped pictures of the room including the stacks of pictures and the ledger sheet and left. He had the parents' phone numbers, so he called Jim Braithwaite. "Jim, it's Jack. Can you meet me at the Dunkin's on Route 13? Yeah, I've found something but I need to keep it quiet. Okay see you in twenty minutes."

"Dear God, I had no idea, Jack. My girls!" Jim was almost in tears.

"Hang in there. If you and I go to Lake Dennison, we may still be able to save them."

"Why just the two of us?"

"Because if I'm wrong, we could end up in jail. Today's political climate is sensitive to children but if don't do this right it could end up being about religious persecution."

"All right. But how do we find them?"

"I took the maps from his apartment. I am not sure why he left them behind, unless he knew where he was going already."

Jim pulled himself together. "He probably didn't want the kids to know how to get back. The less they know, the easier it is to control them."

"Agreed. Time is of the essence. Let me tell at least one person where we are going. The kid's parents are already worried." Jack pulled out his cell and hit a button. "Hello? Jerry? It's Jack Chase."

"Hey Jack. What's up?"

"We have a situation."

"Oh boy, what is it this time?"

"You ever hear of a guy called Pastor Bill?"

"Yeah, we got a notice on him from the FBI as a person of interest. We had a couple of complaints but nothing we could arrest him on. He seems to be quiet most of the time."

"Why does the FBI consider him a person of interest?"

"His name has been linked to some illegal activity, extortion, racketeering and possible kidnapping."

"Do you have his full name?"

"The FBI gave us his aliases, 'William Charles, Walter Preston and Bill Priest. His real name is William Shackelton."

"Thanks Jerry, I will call you later."

"Jack, I know you're an experienced investigator but don't take the law into your own hands. You were lucky once. Don't tempt fate."

"Some kids are missing, Jerry. I'm just trying to get some answers. Talk to you later." Jack hung up his phone and turned to the map. "This is more than the Lake Dennison area. The map is for the whole Birch Hill State Wildlife Management Area."

Jim leaned in for a closer look. "He's circled the parking area at the beginning of the park, the junction of Miller's River and Monadnock Brook, 42°40'24.6"N 72°07'25.8"W, and a small pond at 42°40'49.5"N 72°07'42.9"W. The good thing about the pond is that there's a road near there so it's easy access."

Jim was on edge. "We've camped out here before. If I was going to get away from people but need to have a fast getaway, that's where I'd go."

"All right. Let's drive out there and see what's going on."

"Okay."

The men drove about forty minutes west of Langston. They turned onto Route 202 in Baldwin and passed a Dunkin Donuts. "If we get separated, let's meet at there. It's visible and the only one in the area." Jack was in full investigator mode. "Only if necessary."

"Right." Jim had never been so worried. Jack noticed it. "Jim, we'll find them."

"Alive, I hope. I promise you, Jack if that guy has done anything to them,"

"I understand, Jim but you have to be cool for now. Once we figure out what's going on, we'll turn things over to the police."

Jim grunted as they reached the entrance to Lake Dennison Park. The paved road snaked into the woods and emptied into a large parking lot. There was an access road that led from the lot to the beach and continued into the wooded camping area. "Jack, should we go through the woods or circle around on the paved roads?"

"Going through the woods will give us the element of surprise." Jack had a thought and checked his cell phone. "I suspected as much. No cell service."

"Nuts! How do we call the cops if there's no service?"

"For now, we are on our own. We will go and look. If the kids are not in danger then we will get the police."

Jack started driving up the camping road. The road turned to dirt after the beach and there were puddles. Jack drove carefully through the camping area until they were about 100 yards from the coordinates from the map. Jack got out, threw on his backpack and checked his sidearm. Jim got out and checked his pistol as well. Jack was concerned. "Don't pull that out unless you absolutely have to, okay?"

Jim nodded. "Okay."

The duo crept up through the brush next to the road. They passed an old decrepit school bus and they moved farther off road. They heard some commotion as they got closer. An armed man was leading a bound and blindfolded girl over to an area just out of sight. The girl was crying and appeared frightened. "Shut up and sit down! You are just property so be quiet!" The armed man was looking beyond where he made the girl sit on the ground. A white unmarked moving van pulled up and parked. A slender, bearded man got out of the truck and walked over to the armed man. "Braverman! What is the problem?"

"These kids are getting mouthy. I had to teach a couple of them a lesson."

"You didn't hit them, did you? I can't sell damaged goods!"

"Look Bill,"

"No! You look! I am taking a huge risk here! The feds know I'm in the area and I've got a lot of cash riding on this delivery. It took a long time to get these brats and I don't want any screw ups!"

"All right! All right."

"Get them loaded and ready to move."

The bearded man walked over to the other side of the truck and lit a cigarette. The armed man went over to the clearing and started yelling for people to get up. A few got up almost immediately and a few stumbled and struggled. Braverman called out, "Hey Bill, gimme a hand will ya?" Annoyed, Bill threw the cigarette away and went over to help.

Jack realized that these were his missing students. His blood boiled but he kept his cool. Jim figured it out, too. He whispered loudly. "Jack! He has my girls!"

"I know but we have to keep cool and act fast. They're going to take them away-we have to make sure that truck never leaves here."

"I have an idea." Jim in a moment of inspiration takes out his knife. "Follow   me."
Jim takes the lead and quietly sidles up to the truck. Carefully, he drives the knife into the front tire and the air escapes quickly. The pair dash back into the woods to hide. Once back in hiding, Jack pulls out

a silencer and attaches it to his pistol. He realizes that Jim saw him. "You didn't see that." Jim nodded and smiled. "I'm going to try to do this quietly and without bloodshed. Stay here-I might need backup." Jim agreed and dug in. Jack moved quietly towards the clearing where the kids were being held. They were standing in line, blindfolded with their wrists duct taped together. Jack holstered his weapon and pulled out his knife. He crept over to the last person in line and whispered, "Don't say anything, it's Jack Chase." The girl almost collapsed. "Mr. Chase!"

"Shhhh!" He pulled off her blindfold and cut the tape. "Quietly go that way. Stay out of sight as best you can."

She nodded and darted off. Jack did the same with the next three and realized he was getting close to Braverman. The brute had his rifle slung and was pushing the kids into the truck. Jack decided to circle around and disarm him before Bill discovered that he was there. He moved silently through the thicket and came out about six feet from Braverman. Jack crept up quietly, pulled out his Glock and placed it on the back of Braverman's neck. He said quietly, "Don't move. Take off the rifle." Braverman froze and said, "Hey, Bill you can have a bigger share! It's-" He trailed off when he saw Bill come out of the woods after relieving himself. "Who are you?"

"I said don't move. Gimme the rifle. All right, get on your knees." As Braverman was kneeling, Bill quickly got into the truck and reached for the ignition. Jim appeared at the window with his gun trained on him. He was smiling and holding up the keys. "Get out, now."

Bill got out of the truck and held his hands up. Jim marched him over to Jack and he kneeled down next to Braverman. "Is there anyone else here working with you?"

"Who are you?"

"I'm the Principal. Now answer me."

"No. It's just us."

"What was your plan here? Were you honestly going to sell these kids into slavery?"

The pair remained silent. Jim remembered how angry he was that phony Pastor Bill had kidnapped his girls. "Answer him!" Jim was going to pistol whip him but Jack stopped him. "Jim, untie the kids, I've got this."

Jim glared at the two kneeling men and went to set the kids free. Jack looked at Bill and shook his head. "Am I to assume that you are 'Pastor Bill'?

Bill nodded.

Jack leaned into his face. "What kind of monster, tricks kids and then sells them into slavery?"

With an evil, smug grin, Bill sneered, "A rich one. With good lawyers."

While they were talking, Braverman slowly reaches for his boot knife and hides it in his sleeve. After Jim had released the kids, he came back to Jack. "So how do we get everyone back?"

"I assume they got here in the truck but I think we need to secure these two idiots, first."

Just then, Braverman jumped up and came after Jack. He tackled him to the ground and knocked the gun out of his hand. Jack had been an expert hand to hand combatant so he was able to deflect the knife thrust. After disarming Braverman, the two men fell and wrestled in the mud. Jack used Braverman's weight against him though the men were of about equal size. Jack hit Braverman in the gut and he retaliated with an elbow to the head. Jack was stunned for a moment. Jim was going to assist, but Jack waved him off. "I got this!" Pointing to Pastor Bill "Make sure he doesn't escape!" Jack surprised Braverman with a kick to the knee that dropped him fast. When he rolled over, Braverman's face was just above the knife. He picked up the knife and lunged over on top of Jack. He tried to kill Jack, using the palm of his hand to push it towards Jack's neck. A stone slammed into the side of Braverman's head allowing Jack to push him off. One of the student's that went into the woods came back and saw the commotion. He was a football player named Jeremy Wilson and he wanted revenge. Braverman was still recovering from the blow and the young man had another large rock, intending to crush the kidnapper's skull. Jack stopped him. "No! Jeremy! Put it down!"

"He was going to sell us into slavery! We trusted him!"

"I know! You have every right to be angry but if you kill him, you're no better than he is! Let the authorities deal with him!"

Jeremy was a good kid and realized that Jack was right. He hesitated for a moment then threw the rock away and said, "You aren't worth it". Jack was relieved and looked at Jim. "Get the zip ties. When we get to Dunks, we'll call the state police."

They bound the hands and feet of the men and loaded them into the truck. The kids were rounded up and Jim got them onto the bus. They rode out of the park and down Route 202 to the Dunkin Donuts. Once Jack called the state police, he called Jerry Riggs. "We've found them, Jerry. Just in time, too"

"Where? Here in Langston?"

"No, Lake Dennison in Baldwin. He lured them out there to load them on a truck. Bastards treated them like cattle."

"That's deal with human trafficking. That's all they are to them. You know that's out of my jurisdiction."

"Yes, I know, I've called the State Police. I was hoping you could tell the parents. They've been worried sick for days and I'd like them to know as soon as possible."

"Sure. I'd be glad to do that."

"Thanks."

A few days later, Jack was relaxing over his morning coffee. It was 9:00 am on a Saturday and he had nothing planned. Alma was supposed to drop by around noon and they'd decide what to do. He normally didn't read the newspaper but skimmed the headlines on the computer. He went to thesentinel.com the local newspaper and noticed a headline, "Crusading Principal Rescues Kidnapped Students". Intrigued, he clicked on the story and it was about him and the rescue at Lake Dennison. It was written by a reporter named Mike Chaff:

Crusading Principal Rescues Kidnapped Students

By Mike Chaff

Langston, MA- *Langston High School Principal Jack Chase does it again! The heroic principal and former Army investigator rescued a group of high school students who were sucked into the cult known as, "The Freedom" by a man posing as a minister named Pastor Bill. Most recently, the FBI had classified him as a person of interest and in some part a suspect in some criminal activity to include racketeering, extortion and kidnapping. Now the charge of human trafficking can be added to the list of offenses by the man known as Pastor Bill, aka William Shackelton. Shackelton is a career criminal with a rap sheet as long as your arm. He was the son of a New York gangster and a prostitute. He grew up on the streets but had the demeanor of an academic. He is highly intelligent and briefly attended college on Long Island. When his parents were murdered in a mob hit from a rival gang, he took over his father's empire and ruled it with the same iron fist. After a profitable 5-year run, he was ratted out by a mole within his organization. He was able to hide out for many years, changing his appearance and his name. Shackelton had a flair for the theatrical, and used that to his advantage by impersonating, clergy, psychiatrists and other white-collar professionals to evade capture. He never stayed in one place for very long and discovered the dark industry of human trafficking. Shackelton became a ghost and allegedly moved his victims between the US and Europe. Several of his victims escaped and most reported their harrowing experience to the FBI. They began to track his where-abouts for several years, but he was as slippery as they come. It wasn't until the intrepid Principal Chase, a former Army investigator turned educator crossed his path and took him down. It is believed that Shackelton was a key player in a much larger cartel.*

Jack was surprised the reporter knew so much about Shackelton, but gave it little thought. The article went on and Jack decided that he'd read the rest of it later. He had just taken the last swig of his coffee when his phone rang. "Hello?"

"Good Morning, Mr. Chase. My name is George Stanton from the Boston FBI office."

"What can I do for you, Mr. Stanton?"

"I'll be direct. We need to get a statement from you about the incident."

"Okay, when?"

"As soon as possible. Monday morning at your office? Say 9am?

"Make it 9:30 if you don't mind."

"Not at all. Myself and another agent will meet you at 9:30am."

"Why two agents?"

"Standard procedure. We like to buddy up our agents for safety."

"Makes sense. See you Monday morning."

"Very good. Thank you, Mr. Chase."

"No problem."

Jack's interest was piqued enough at this point to google Shackelton. He found an article on him from about ten years ago. A reporter doing a story about organized crime families from New York and New Jersey had interviewed Shackelton. He was asking him about the effects of organized crime on the next generation of the families involved. Shackelton's responses were calculated and chilling. He spoke about his childhood abuse and witnessing his father's cruelty. He described his mother as either too cold or too afraid to get close to him, should she incur his father's wrath. When Shackelton was twelve, his mother convinced his father to allow him to go to boarding school upstate. Though saddened that she sent him away, he viewed this as his mother trying to protect him. It had worked because about 6 months after, both of his parents were gunned down in cold blood. Shackelton was devastated and even mentioned that he probably would have gone into a legitimate profession if his parents had not been murdered in such a cold fashion. He was interested in becoming a doctor or even a priest but whatever kind feelings for mankind he had died with his mother. He decided that he would take over his father's empire and use it to avenge his parents. It took him three years to find those responsible, both the rival mob boss that gave the order and the assassins that carried it out. Shackelton did not like killing as a rule, but he made sure that the deaths of those men were exceptionally brutal.

Shackelton admitted he had a love of theatre. He often used disguises and would lead operations from the front, earning him a significant amount of respect from his men. He seemed to treat his women well. He was even going to retire from organized crime when his legitimate businesses were doing well. Shackelton was in the process of quietly closing down operations when his main warehouse of stolen loot was raided. It seemed a few of his men wanted to take over the family business so they ratted him out. After a lengthy court trial, the only charges that stuck were racketeering, illegal gambling, and fraud. Since Shackelton had no prior record he was sentenced to 10 to 15 years at Devens Federal Penitentiary, with parole in five years. Shackelton was a model prisoner and was released in 7 years for good behavior. Once released he dropped out of sight.

Jack was lost in thought when he heard his front door open. It was Alma. "Hey Stud."

"Hey Babe." He didn't look up. Alma saw the look on his face. "Whatcha' reading?"

"Oh, I was just reading about this guy Shackelton."

"Is that that 'Pastor Bill' guy that tried to take the kids?"

"Yeah."

Alma shivered. "Ugh. That guy gives me the creeps. I hope they put him away for a long time."

"Me too. Human trafficking is a real political hot button right now."

"Sure is. You apparently got the Governor's attention."

"What?"

"Take a look." Alma took out her phone and showed Jack the Twitter feed:

#massgovernorjamesbrattle Another win for justice! Jack Chase, the Defender of the Innocent strikes another blow against evil! Well done, Jack! #justiceiscool, #votebrattlechase2020.

"Social media. I'm not sure I'll ever understand it."

Alma squeezed in between Jack and his desk to sit on his lap. "My Hero!" Alma swoons comically and he tickles her. "Stop! Mr. Defender!"

"You make me sound like a lawyer."

"The kids think you're a hero. As do a lot of their parents."

"You know me, nobody messes with my kids."

They hear the sound of a car pulling up. "Speaking of your kids, I think I hear one now."

The door swings open and Courtney and her boyfriend Derek come in. "Hi, Dad!"

"Sweetie Pie!" Jack got up from his chair and hugged his daughter. "I didn't know you were coming today!"

"Yeah, well after the media swarm, I thought I'd better come in for moral support."

"I'm just glad to see you. Hi Derek." Jack held out his hand and Derek shook it.

"Hi, Mr. Chase."

Courtney was gushing with pride. "Plus, I wanted to tell you in person how proud I am of you. You are every bit the Defender of the Innocent."

"You saw the governor's tweet?"

"Can't help it. It's blowing up everywhere."

"Ah, crap."

"Dad, you can't do amazing things in secret forever. People will notice."

"I suppose. I just want my kids to be safe."

"Believe me I know. You are every bit the obnoxious, overprotective father you claimed to be."

"You know, it takes a special skill to be that obnoxious." Everyone laughed. Courtney nuzzled her father's neck. "One more thing,"

"What's that, Sweetheart?"

Courtney looked at Jack, beaming, "Mom, would be proud of you, too."

"Thanks, Honey."

Monday came fast and Jack was in his office by 7am as per usual. He checked his calendars for the week, both paper and digital. Jack still felt more comfortable with a day planner but with Courtney's help he was able to manage the calendar app on his phone. He found that linking it with her and now with Alma's phone, he kept his appointments pretty well. He glanced down at the reminder and remembered the meeting with the FBI agents. Nothing else was on the day's calendar, so he did his morning rounds and grabbed a coffee in the teacher's lounge. He shuffled papers and remembered he wanted to get an early start on next year's budget. He set up the papers when Alma, buzzed him on the intercom. "Mr. Chase, your 9:30 appointment is here."

Jack always smiled when Alma called him, 'Mr. Chase' at work. It was common knowledge that they were dating so it was a bit of a private joke. He looked up as the two well-dressed people entered his office and closed the door. "Mr. Chase, I'm George Stanton. This is Agent Amy Tasker."

Jack invited them to sit down. "Good Morning. So, what I can do for the FBI?"

Both agents sat down. Stanton spoke first. "Mr. Chase, I get right to the point. We need your help."

Jack raised an eyebrow. "You need my help? What on earth for?"

"You work on the Hanney case caught our attention. You handled it like a professional investigator."

"I was a CID investigator when I was in the Army. But you knew that already."

Tasker spoke plainly. "Yes, and it seems you were pretty formidable during that time, too."

"Look, I retired out the Army and got into education. I'm happy here and I enjoy what I do."

"We understand and we are not asking you to change anything, yet. You had a run in recently with William Shackelton. We've had him under surveillance for a long time."

"You guys knew what he was doing?"

"Yes. We kept our distance."

Jack got angry and interrupted Tasker. "You mean to tell me you knew what was going on? Did you know that that bastard tried to hurt my kids? I had to stop one of my kids from bashing his skull and that wasn't easy! Where the hell were you guys when this was happening?"

"Calm down, Mr. Chase. What we are telling you is that we knew what he was doing, we just didn't know where. Had we found him before you did, we would not be here."

"All right, fine. Again, why do you need my help?"

"The reason Shackelton was under surveillance is that we believe he is a small part of a much larger, international organization."

"I thought he was some big crime boss?"

"He was, once. His empire crumbled when he went to jail. There was only enough evidence to put him away for fifteen years. Shackelton made parole in seven. Once he got out, he tried to re-establish his organization but his contacts had scattered and he had no resources. He operated small time for two years until he was connected with the death of a young nun near Boston. Are you familiar with the Sister Mary Atwell Case?"

"Yeah, I read about that case. Three years ago, her body was found in a ditch behind an abandoned gas station in Waltham."

Tasker stood up and paced as she talked. "She was living in Water-town. She was teaching at an all-girls catholic school, St. Baskins. She only lived five minutes away from the school."

Jack leaned back in his chair. "If memory serves, she had gone out shopping for an engagement gift for her younger sister and disappeared. They found her three months later in mid-March. Time of death was mid-December. There was a lot snow that year. Cause of death was blunt force trauma to the head."

Tasker continued. "Sister Mary was about to leave St. Baskins because she felt that the Catholic church was out of touch with society. She had asked the Archdiocese to consider letting teach in the public-school system. They refused. Mary was young, bright and full of promise. She loved her students and she was very protective of them."

"Such a shame. I probably would have hired her here."

"Several nuns thought she was murdered because she found out that the head priest was sexually abusing the girls."

"Was that guy the School administrator?"

"Yes, his name was Father A. Joseph Halloran."

"I remember that."

Stanton took his turn. "Halloran had been at the school for three years. He has raised some suspicion due to his flamboyant style and strict dis-cipline. Some of his 'disciplinary' methods were questionable. Halloran would meet girls alone in his office. He chose to make his office on the other side of school away from the main office."

Jack raised an eyebrow. "That's inefficient. Did he meet parents there, too?"

"To our knowledge, he hardly ever met with parents; when he did, he would talk to them on the phone and rarely. Other questionable acts were parties he hosted for the kids. Mixers he called them. He said they were to help the girls prepare for college. Usually, older men would be there to talk about 'college opportunities'. They were always after school. We believe they were grooming them for the sex ring."

Jack didn't skip a beat. "Let me guess. Some of the girls were not the same after these mixers."

Tasker sounded tense. "Several of them had complained about the men at these parties. Halloran would insist that the girls, some of them fourteen or fifteen, go into another room with the door closed for a 'private college consultation'. Halloran or another priest would stand at the door. Several witnesses watched the girls come out of the room and go right out of the building. Some would sit by themselves."

"I highly doubt they were talking about college."

"We agree. Three of the girls," Tasker started to tear up. "Three of those girls committed suicide. All within a month of these meetings."

Jack was surprised to see such emotion from a government agent. "Agent Tasker?"

"One of them was my niece. We were close."

"Close enough to question whether or not it was an actual suicide?"

"Bethany was a sweet girl. Naïve but very smart. She had grown up in the Catholic church and trusted them. I had my doubts about a lot of things they did."

Stanton patted Tasker on the shoulder and invited her to sit back down. "Mr. Chase, we want you to go undercover. We want you to pose as a priest at St. Baskins."

"You want me to go undercover at an all-girls catholic school?"

"Yes. As you know the Catholic church has great influence and wields a lot of power. We can't get a court order to get into the school unless something significant has happened. We haven't been able to make a direct connection between Halloran, Atwell or the suicides."

"Finding the corpse of a dead nun isn't significant?" Jack was pensive.

"Had she been found on school property, that would have made it a crime scene. THAT would have made it significant." Stanton furrowed his brow.

Jack stood up and walked to the window, overlooking the front driveway. "So, let me see if I got this right. You want me to pose as a priest, at a Catholic girl's school and do what exactly?"

"Casually interview some students and faculty. Nose around and find something that we can use to connect Halloran and expose his network. You know the school environment and we can secure credentials for you."

"Right, so what does this have to do with Shackelton?"

The two agents looked at each other. "We're almost certain that Halloran is supplying Shackelton with girls."

"Okay, that's a stretch."

"Not as much as you think. When Shackelton was in prison, he wanted to see a priest. As is with all prisoners, he was entitled to religious counsel. Guess who showed up?"

"Halloran, obviously."

"Right. Shackelton had requested Halloran by name. He was his childhood priest, allegedly. He came up from New Jersey on a number of occasions."

"No one thought that strange?"

"At that point, no one had suspected Halloran of anything, but once Shackelton was released from Devens, Halloran requested a transfer up to a Boston area archdiocese."

"That's a lot of devotion to a single parishioner. You think Halloran recruited Shackelton to get him girls?"

"Possibly, or Shackelton was able to reestablish his ring and Halloran stumbled in to an opportunity. We don't know who approached who but we're pretty sure that they are working together."

"All right. You have my interest. I will have to discuss it with my family first."

Stanton lowered his voice. "Mr. Chase, there's one thing you have to know."

"What's that?"

"Halloran is connected throughout the area. He's not just the school administrator. He's the Police and Fire Chaplain for the region, he's the senior civilian liaison chaplain for the Mass National Guard and he has the support of the Boston Archdiocese. You must tread lightly."

"Understood."

The agents stood up. Stanton seemed to relax. "Excellent. You have 24 hours. Whether or not you decide to help, give us a call." Stanton handed Jack his card. "Remember some of these young girls are the same age as the students here. Think about it."

Jack walked them outside and shook their hands. He went back into the outer office. "Alma, you got a minute?"

Alma nodded and followed him into his office. "You are not going to believe this."

"What is it? Are they trying to recruit you for the FBI?"

"Not exactly. They want me to go undercover."

Alma reacted loudly. "WHAT? What do you mean undercover?"

"Shhhh! Honey, please!"

"Sorry. Why on earth do they want you to go undercover?"

"The need to find evidence to investigate Halloran. Or at least enough to get a search warrant."

"Why on earth for?"
"The short version is that they suspect Shackelton and a priest of trafficking young girls."

"What school are you going to?

"St. Baskins Prep in Watertown. I haven't decided if I'm doing this."

Alma smiled wryly. "Of course, you are, Jack Chase. If Shackelton is the tip of the iceberg, you won't be satisfied until you take them all down. It's just who you are."

A week later, a black rental car pulled into the faculty parking lot at St. Baskins. Jack tugged at the unfamiliar priest's collar and took a breath. He wasn't usually nervous on a case but the stakes were different this time. The lives of young girls, children, were at stake. Jack didn't grow up Catholic so he had to learn a lot of the customs in a short time. He decided to make his character, Fr. Philip Stevens, as nerdy and awkward as he could to cover some of the gaps in his knowledge. It had been a long time since he had gone undercover so he had to rely on his instincts and his wits. Jack got out of his car and headed for the front office. There was no door access panel like at Langston High. No bubble camera, no intercom. Jack just walked in and found the office straight ahead. He stepped in the office and felt strangely at home. The receptionist had a beehive hairdo and an outfit from 1962. As Jack looked around, the décor hadn't changed much since then. "Ahem, Good Morning." The woman looked up and was startled. "Oh! Father! I didn't see you there."

"Yes, my name is Father Philip Stevens."

"The new English teacher! We weren't expecting you until next week! My name is Moira Sanders and if you will give me a moment, I can show you around."

"That would be lovely, Sister Sanders."

"Oh, we're not too formal around here, Father. You can call me Moira." Moira leaned in, "We save the 'Sister' stuff for the nuns!" Moira chuckled with a snort. "Follow me." Moira locked her computer and pulled the shade down on the receptionist's window. "The girls all know I've stepped away when the shade is down."

"I see. How are the girls here?"

"Oh, they are wonderful. Well-heeled and well behaved. This area is very affluent. We're very fortunate. We get students from Belmont, Arlington, Newton, Cambridge and even some out of state."

"Out of state? Do they commute?"

"No. We have some local dormers. We've repurposed an old convent in Waltham, St. Benedict's. It's about 15 minutes away so we have to shuttle the girls here and back every day. They go home on weekends if it's a reasonable distance."

"Reminds me of being in the military. I enjoyed my time when I was a chaplain's assistant down in New Jersey at Fort Monmouth."

"I've never been to New Jersey!"

"It's very pretty. I recommend the north east area to start. Beautiful homes and towns make it idyllic. They love to tend their lawns and gardens. Status and such."

The two continued in small talk as the went towards the teacher's lounge. The walls were lined with a plethora of Catholic imagery. Small statues of Mary, Jesus on the Cross and everything in between. Various saints were scattered throughout the building, patron saints of anything and everything. Mary stopped at an unassuming door. "Here we are! Would you like a cup of coffee, Father?"

"I'd love one, thank you."

Moira went over to the Keurig and pulled two pods out. "How do you take it?"

"Regular, please. Or flavored creamer if you have it."

"It'll be ready in a minute."

"That's great, thanks."

Another teacher came in. He was grumbling and using some un-priest-like language. "Can you believe those little bitches!"

"Father Blake! What's the problem?" Moira was very concerned.

"Martha Benson! She has no respect for anyone!"

"What did she do?"

"Somehow she doctored pictures of me and Sister Elise and put us in highly pornographic positions! She posted them on the school web-site!"

Jack spoke up, "Who controls the website?"

"We have the students make content mostly but it has to be approved by Father Halloran."

Moira set her coffee aside and went over to a desk. She pulled out several pieces of paper and brought them to Father Blake. "Okay, you know the drill. Also set if you can send me those pictures. They're timestamped so we'll figure out how this all happened. I notify Father Halloran."

"Thanks, Moira. I'll tell you I really regret going into teaching some-times!"

As Blake left, Jack knew how he felt. But he was also concerned about how Blake interacted with the students. He had had a few Catholic school transfers back in Langston but they typically enjoy the freedom of a public school. More freedom, less strict environment. Moira came back over to the Keurig and finished making her coffee. "That man needs to retire."

"Why do you say that?"

"He's lost his passion, I think. He came here about ten years ago, about the same time I did. I was going to school to become a teacher and they needed a teacher's assistant. Things worked out and the offered me a position as office manager and receptionist. It was slightly better than a teacher's salary so I took it. I'm glad I did."

"Father Blake was happier, then?"

"He was actually looking for an 'end of career' job. He had been in the same parish for about 30 years and then there were some complaints."

"Oh?"

"Yes, they weren't like what you hear in the news. The complaint was that he was harsh with a number of parishioners and that he would talk about what he heard in confession."

Jack knew that was a serious offense. "Oh, dear."

Moira continued. "Plus, the other problem is the Father Halloran doesn't care for him much. I never understood why. He's a nice enough man but I don't think the priesthood was his calling."

"I can understand that. I've had my doubts, crises of faith and the like."

"Yes, I think we all do. Well, there is not much time before lunch so let me show you around some more."

Jack and Moira continued for about an hour. The stopped in the English wing. "This is your classroom. Father Malone is finishing up this week, so I'll ask him if he's willing to let you audit the class tomorrow and Friday."

"That would be wonderful. When will I meet Father Halloran?"

"Probably tomorrow. He is in Boston at the Archdioceses meeting with the Cardinal about additional funding. Our budget gets cut every year, but somehow Father Halloran is able to find more money. He's a God-send! Pun fully intended!" Moira giggled and snorted again.

Jack changed out of his priest's vestments and left St. Baskins. Since Halloran wasn't around, he left early and drove around the area near the school. It was a 45-minute drive back to Langston so Jack had plenty of time to think. Stanton had given him a copy of the Atwell case file, both digital and hard copies. Jack decided to open the large envelope and look up the address of the old gas station near where Sister Mary's body was found. Jack pulled up to the abandoned station and there was a construction fence around it. A power station was a few hundred feet east of the station. He parked at a Nazarene church across the street and got out. He followed the fence around to the ease-ment and crawled through a gap. There was a lot of growth but there was a worn pathway to the ditch. He thought that strange until he came to a clearing. The ditch was beyond the clearing but someone had de-liberately cleared a small area. The area was unusually well kept and Jack realized why. Near a tree in the small clearing, there were hun-dreds of cards, teddy bears, candles, and notes. All addressed to Sister Mary Atwell. Someone had made a shrine. Jack looked at the notes and cards. Some were homemade, others purchased from a store. Most were not signed but many of them had a common symbol. It was a round lattice pattern with praying hands in the middle. There were a few necklaces hung around a nob on the tree that had the same symbol in cardboard and leather. Jack took out his cell phone and took several pictures. He knew that symbols had meanings when they appeared of-ten in a case. Jack looked around some more and found where Mary's body had lay. He compared it to the file pictures and noted the signif-icant details. He went back to his car and looked at the photos. He decided to mull it over as he drove home. He also didn't want to draw too much attention to himself in case he had to come back.

Jack finally arrived home with more questions than answers. He treated his cassock like a dress suit since he had to go back tomorrow. After steaming the outfit, he heated up some leftovers and sat at the dining table. He had time alone since Alma was out with her sister and Courtney was up in New Hampshire, helping her grandmother. Jack took out his laptop and it placed on the table. He decided to review the Sister Mary Atwell case file while he ate. He went and got the file folder and sat back down. He took out the thumb drive with all the case documents and copied them to his hard drive. Jack's eyes were drawn to the photo of an attractive young woman. He studied the woman's face and felt a little sad for her. "So much promise. What a waste," he thought. Jack went on to read the file:

SISTER MARY ATWELL

Born June 30, 1990, Disappeared December 5, 2017 (Age 27)

Body discovered March 16, 2018

Cause of death: Intracerebral hemorrhage caused by skull fracture

Background: Mary Atwell was born in Troy, NY. She attended Sacred Heart Catholic School on Spring Avenue and Catholic Central High School, both in Albia. She was valedictorian of her Catholic high school class in 2008, where she had also been the May Queen and the president of the senior class and student council.

She attended Williams College in North Adams, MA and graduated with a Bachelor's of Arts, having a double major in Secondary Education and English Literature. Sister Mary then attained a Master's in Education Administration from the University of Massachusetts, Amherst. She student taught at Our Lady of Perpetual Mercy in Amherst, MA during her senior year. She then taught for two years at St. Leo's Elementary school in Leominster and then arrived at St. Baskins in 2016.

DISAPPEARANCE AND DEATH

At the time she disappeared, Atwell taught at St. Baskins Preparatory High School in Watertown, Massachusetts as a drama and English Literature teacher. On December 5, 2017, she left the apartment she shared with fellow teacher and friend Sister Elizabeth Antonia Cravello at the Arsenal Apartments, 465 Arsenal St, Watertown, en route to the Colonial Shopping Center to purchase a gift at Elliott's Jeweler for her sister's engagement. Records indicate Atwell cashed a paycheck at Watertown Savings Bank, 60 Main St. that night and possibly made a purchase at The Danish Pastry House, 205 Arlington St, since a box of muffins was found in the front seat of Atwell's car. The car, a 2011 Toyota Corolla, in muddy condition, was found by Cravello's friends, the priests Peter McCall and David L. Book. The car was found illegally parked across from her apartment complex at 4:40 the next morning. Residents of Arsenal Apartments spotted Atwell in her car at approximately 8:30 that night, and others spotted her car illegally parked across the street around two hours later. It is believed that when Atwell's body was found, she had been deceased for at least two months, maybe longer. The heavy snowfall and frigid temperatures had slowed decomposition almost to preservation.

Police searched the area immediately following Atwell's disappearance but did not find her. On March 16, 2018, her body was found by a Massachusetts Electric lineman, in a dry swamp located along an easement behind a closed gas station on the 1400 block of Trapelo Road, in a residential area of Waltham. An autopsy performed by Deputy Medical Examiner William Kosloski revealed that Atwell died from an intracerebral hemorrhage following a fracture to her skull from a blow to her left temple by a blunt instrument. The case remains unsolved.

BACKGROUND

During Atwell's tenure at St. Baskins High School, it was alleged that two of the priests, Fathers Joseph Halloran and Neil McHenry, were sexually abusing the girls at the school in addition to trafficking them to others. In 2019, Pamela Croton and Jennifer Stone, former students at St. Baskins claimed to have been sexually abused by Halloran. The families filed a lawsuit against Halloran, McHenry, the school, the Archdiocese, and Bishop Turner. The trial court dismissed the due to a lack of evidence. Plaintiffs appealed. A writ of certiorari was granted by the Court of Appeals of The Commonwealth which upheld the lower court decision.

Jack was fascinated. The head detective on the case was Mark Brown from the Middlesex District Attorney's Office, Division of Investigative Services, Massachusetts State Police. Brown took extensive notes, both audio and typed. He digitized everything but still kept hardcopies. The case notes took on almost s surreal life of their own. Brown interviewed a several of the girls and made audio recordings. Fortunately, those were on the thumb drive with everything else. When Jack opened up the main folder on the drive, he found a few folders that caught his attention. The first was 'Audio Interviews Group 1', the second, 'Audio Interviews Group 2', and a third folder, named the same way. He clicked on the first folder and there were more folders inside with girl's names. Each subfolder had a few dozen individual mp3 files. Jack saw the folder marked, 'Pamela Croton'. He clicked on the first file and the audio started to play:

Brown: Interview number one. February 27, 2019. This is Detective Mark Brown interviewing Miss Pamela Croton, aged 17. Miss Croton, may I call you Pamela?"

Pamela: "Yes."

Brown: "Just for the record, Pamela, will you confirm that you are not performing under duress?"

Pamela: "I don't know what that means."

Brown: "It means that you are answering questions without me forcing you or threatening you. You're doing it because you want to, of your own free will."

Pamela: "Yes, that's true. I need to tell someone."

Brown: "Okay. Remember that you can tell me as much as you want. If you feel anxious or overwhelmed and you want to stop just let me know. But also know that sometimes, answers lead to other questions, okay? Take as much time as you want."

Pamela: "Thank you."

Brown: "All right. Pamela tell me about Father Halloran."

Pamela: "When I first started going to St. Baskins, I went into confessional. Everyone had to, every week. We had to keep a journal of all of our church activities and if we felt that we had done something wrong, we would have to put that in the journal, too. One weekend in the fall, my uncle Charlie was visiting from Michigan. He was my mother's youngest sibling. He was twenty and I was only 13. My mother thought we would get along since we were close in age. At least she thought so. That weekend, we went out to the Quabbin Reservoir to go camping. We ended up sharing a tent and he, ah (faltering) woke me up by climbing into my sleeping bag."

Brown: "You folks were okay with this?"

Pamela: "They didn't know. They had stayed in town with some friends while we camped out."

Brown: "What happened next?"

Pamela: "When Charlie was in the bag, he had gotten his pants down, and pulled mine down, too. I was nervous but I still didn't know what was happening until he, (begins to cry) he,"

Brown: "I understand, you don't have to say it."

Pamela: "When he, did that to me, I screamed. He put his hand over my mouth, and said, 'this is just between us. Don't you dare tell anyone else!' I felt awful, like I was going to throw up."

Brown: "Pamela, I am so sorry this happened to you. No one should have to go through that."

Pamela: "Thanks. I wish I could say that was the end of it. Right after that I went to confession at St. Baskins and I wrote it in my diary. I didn't know that Father Halloran was in the confessional so I told him everything. He said to follow up with him with counseling in his office. The next day, I was in math class and I was called down to his office. I was a little nervous but I thought he was going to help me."

Brown: "What did he say to you?"

Pamela: "The first time he talked to me, he told me that good Catholic girls don't have that happen to them. He said that he really wanted to help me be a good Catholic girl. He said (getting agitated) that I must have done something to encourage it! I started to get even more confused. Then, he started rubbing my shoulders, then he said, 'I need to check you, to see how you are developing. He touched and rubbed my thigh and then he touched my privates."

Brown: "How often did he touch you?"

Pamela: "At first, it was only a couple of times a week. Then after a while, he was always calling me down to his office."

The audio ended at that point. Jack could feel his fury for this Father Halloran. He felt so bad for Pamela. He snapped out if it and clicked on the next mp3 file.

Brown: "Follow up notes on Interview One with Pamela Croton. She used her journal to track everything that happened, once Halloran began having her in his office. She told me that she had confided in Sister Mary Atwell and Sister Margaret, the history teacher. She recalled that one day, a few weeks after Halloran started called her to his office, Sister Mary Atwell once came to her and said gently, "Are the priests hurting you?" This surprised Pamela and she broke down crying. Sister Mary brought her to the teachers' lounge and spoke with her privately. Sister Mary had voiced her suspicions and started to craft a plan to protect her. Later Pamela found out about several girls who were being molested by Halloran and Father Neil McHenry. One of the other girls was Jennifer Stone. Both women have said that she (Atwell) was the only one who helped them and the other girls abused by Halloran; they believe that she was murdered prior to discussing the matter with the Archdiocese of Boston. Unfortunately, there is no evidence for this assertion.

Jack clicked on a folder called, 'Halloran". The folder had enough files to fill the screen. He clicked on the first file, also an mp3. It was named, 'Entry 1':

Brown: "Currently, there is no physical evidence linking Halloran to this investigation. That said, it was revealed in late 2016 that the Archdiocese had paid off numerous settlements to Halloran's alleged victims since 2011. Halloran had been moved around approximately every three years but the Archdiocese refused to say why. Pamela Croton alleges that, two and a half months before Atwell's body was discovered, and only a day or two after Atwell disappeared on December 5, Halloran drove her to a wooded site near what he told her was Hanscom

Air Force Base, Lexington, Mass and showed her the body. Croton claims to remember trying repeatedly to brush off the black marks on Atwell's face while frantically repeating the words, "Help me, help me." Croton's account was brought into question by scientific evidence showing that when the body was initially examined the face was clean. However, Dr. Timothy Brennan, the pathologist who worked on the case with Dr. William Kosloski, later confirmed that there had been gun powder residue in the victim's mouth when found. There were also teeth missing and legions in the mouth that were more noticeable when the body achieved room temperature. Oddly enough, there were no gunshot wounds of any kind on Atwell's body."

"Oh, dear Lord, that poor girl." Jack thought. He clicked on the next file. Brown's tone of voice was less formal

Brown: "Halloran is an oily bastard. The archdiocese is tight-lipped and they won't release anything. It's damned frustrating. Next entry. Croton alleged that when Halloran brought her out to see the body, he reportedly told her, "You see what happens when you say bad things about good people?" Croton was so frightened that she was sick and out of school for the next week. When she returned, her meetings with Halloran resumed.

Jack looked in the same folder and saw a document named Final Resting Place. He clicked on it and read:

Several days after Atwell's disappearance, on December 19, 2017, the body of Janice Marston, a 25-year-old woman who looked like Mary Atwell, was discovered by a utility worker in the same wooded location where Halloran had allegedly driven Croton to see Atwell's body. Atwell's body was not found until March 16, 2018 and its discovery was not in the wooded location near Hanscom A.F. Base but in the dried swamp bed behind a closed gas station in Waltham.

Jack looked at the clock and two hours had passed. He didn't want to make it a late night, but he did see a folder named, 'Janice Marston'. He decided to leave that on for tomorrow. He pulled out a pad and wrote, 'left off with Janice' to remind him of where to start next time.

Morning came fast and Jack had to get to Watertown. He rolled out of bed at 5:30am. He put on the priest's cassock and checked himself in the mirror. When he got into his car, he sent Alma a good morning text and said he'd talk to her that night. Jack pulled out his wallet and took out a twenty for lunch. He locked the wallet and his cell phone in the glove compartment and turned on his burner phone. He didn't want anyone to get suspicious so he followed his old protocol for going undercover. Nothing that would compromise his identity was on his body. He pulled on to Lancaster Ave and headed toward Route 2. Once he merged onto the highway, Jack let his mind wander. "What does Janice Marston have to do Mary Atwell? Were they friends? Was she a student that had been molested by Halloran or McHenry? Why was she killed?" Jack realized that he had come up with more questions than he had answers. He pulled into the school and walked through the lobby to the office. Moira was on the phone and waved him in. He passed the window and went in the door. Jack saw a packet with the name 'Fr. Stevens. He looked at the clock. It was 6:55. He opened the packet and there was a welcome letter and two schedules. One of the schedules was his own teaching schedule and the other was the Daily Bell Schedule. He set aside the letter and studied the Bell schedule:

Daily Bell Schedule

First Bell   7:15

Morning Mass   7:20 – 7:45

Confession   7:50 – 8:00

1st Period	8:08 – 8:48
2nd Period	8:52 – 9:32
3rd Period	9:36 – 10:16
4th Period	10:20 – 11:00
5th Period	11:04 – 11:44
First Lunch Period	11:50 – 12:10
Second Lunch Period	12:15 – 12:35
6th Period	12:40 – 1:20
7th Period	1:25 – 2:05
8th Period	2:10 – 2:40

Jack read the welcome letter. It was on official school letterhead:

Saint Baskins Preparatory School

770 Mt Oxford St

Watertown, MA 02472

www.stbaskinsprep.com

Dear Father Stevens,

We are delighted to have you join our staff here at St. Baskins. You come highly recommended by the Archdiocese and we look forward to having you here. There are just a few things to remember. The staff is expected on time so we start each day promptly. Morning Mass is critical, as it sets the tone for the day. We are committed to making sure that each student has a firm faith in our Lord, and we achieve this by daily prayer and confession. You are scheduled to receive student confession after the first week.

We pride ourselves for being 'old school' with a modern attitude. We are open to many new methods of teaching our students while maintain a rich tradition in the Catholic faith. Should you have any ideas, comments or concerns, please let me know.

In His Service,

Father A. Joseph Halloran

School Administrator

Jack put the papers back in the large brown envelope and looked at the clock. It was 7:08. "Moira, forgive me. Which way to the chapel?"

"No problem, Father. Just go past the nurse's office, down the stairs, left and then right. That'll bring you in the back way. If all else fails, follow the kids."

"Thank you, Moira. I'll see you later."

Jack walked down towards the nurse's office. He glanced in the room and saw a girl sitting on the examination bench holding herself as if she were cold. He would normally go in and console a student but he had to maintain his cover. He quickly memorized her face as he continued to the chapel. Jack got to the bottom of the stairs and turned left then right. Other than a handicapped bathroom, the hallway brought him to the chapel. Jack emerged next to the altar. He was tempted to sit at the back but he realized the priests are always up front. He sat down next to two other priests as the students filed in. Once the chapel was full, the priest closest to the lectern stood up and addressed the congregation. "All rise." In an eerie unison everyone stood up at once. The priest held his hands up over the congregation and began:

Halloran: In the name of the Father, and of the Son, and of the Holy Spirit.

Congregation: Amen

Halloran: The grace of our Lord Jesus Christ, and the love of God, and the communion of the Holy Spirit be with you all.

Congregation: And with your spirit

Halloran: Brethren, let us acknowledge our sins, and so prepare ourselves to celebrate the sacred mysteries.

Congregation: I confess to almighty God and to my sisters, that I have greatly sinned, in my thoughts and in my words, in what I have done and in what I have failed to do, And, striking my breast, they say: through my fault, through my fault, through my most grievous fault; therefore I ask blessed Mary ever-Virgin, all the Angels and Saints, and you, my brothers and sisters, to pray for me to the Lord our God.

Halloran: May almighty God have mercy on you, forgive you your sins, and bring us to everlasting life.

Congregation: Amen. Glory to God in the highest, and on earth peace to people of good will.

We praise you,

we bless you,

we adore you,

we glorify you,

we give you thanks for your great glory,

Lord God, heavenly King,

O God, almighty Father.

Lord Jesus Christ, Only Begotten Son,

Lord God, Lamb of God, Son of the Father,

you take away the sins of the world,

have mercy on us;

you take away the sins of the world,

receive our prayer;

you are seated at the right hand of the Father,

have mercy on us.

For you alone are the Holy One,

you alone are the Lord,

you alone are the Most High,

Jesus Christ,

with the Holy Spirit, the Virgin Mary

in the glory of God, the Father.

Amen.

The congregation remained standing. Jack noticed the lack of emotion in the congregation. Most of the girls kept their heads and eyes down. Halloran continued.

Halloran: Let us pray. May the Lord bless your minds, bodies and spirits. Deliver you from temptation, and protect you from evil. In the name of the Father, the Son and the Holy Spirit.

Congregation: In the name of the Father, Son, and Holy Spirit, Amen." The girls crossed themselves robotically and sat down.

Jack noticed that there were three priests, including himself. He surmised that the priest presiding over mass was Halloran. "Good Morning, Students."

The congregation replied, "Good Morning, Father Halloran."

"As you know, Father Malone is leaving us. He has been asked by the Archdiocese to take over a parish in Salem. As we will miss him, he will also be the Campus Catholic Liaison to Salem State University. We are glad that he will still be involved in education. We have a few graduating seniors starting there in the fall, so you folks make sure to connect with him." The priest put up one hand and prayed. All the girls stood. "May the Lord, our God bless and keep him. Amen." Everyone sat again. "I will read from the Old Testament, the book of Judges:

And it came to pass in those days, when there was no king in Israel, that there was a certain Levite sojourning on the side of mount Ephraim, who took to him a concubine out of Bethlehemjudah.

And his concubine played the whore against him, and went away from him unto her father's house to Bethlehemjudah, and was there four whole months.

And his father in law, the damsel's father, retained him; and he abode with him three days: so, they did eat and drink, and lodged there."

Halloran continued. "Let it be known that the Levite was led into temptation to lay with the concubine, that the Levite was led astray. He was led astray by the temptation of a loose woman!" The priest paused, dramatically to let that sink in. "A vile, deceitful harlot! As you know, I take the development of our young ladies here at St. Baskins very seriously. Each one of our staff are committed to guiding you to a full and productive life. That said, I am somewhat disappointed to hear that some of you have been engaging in immoral activities that will jeopardize their futures. A few of you used a computer to do some horrible things. I know who you are and you are scheduled for counseling within the next few days. Make sure all of you attend confessional before lunch. All rise."

The congregation stood up. Halloran again raised his hands toward the congregation. "Go in peace, glorifying the Lord by your life."

Congregation: "May the peace of the Lord be with you."

Halloran: "You are dismissed."

Jack got up with the other two priests and began to file out through the back. Jack lingered and introduced himself to the other priests. Father Halloran came out last. He strode with a swagger that was unusual for a man of the cloth. He stuck out his hand and Jack took it. "You must be Father Stevens! I am so glad you came for morning mass. It's one of my favorite times of the day. I think it's important to start the day off with some inspiration and some clarity, don't you?"

"Oh yes! Yes, it's very important."

"Splendid! Well then! I am off to teach ethics class. We'll talk more at the college mixer after school." A without hesitation, Halloran turned on his heel and moved down the hall. The word 'mixer' put Jack on edge. He knew he had to get to the bottom of things fast.

Jack checked his class schedule and found the classroom. He was still observing so he didn't have to do a lesson plan. He walked into the room and found Father Malone sitting at his desk. "Father Malone?"

"Yes! Hello, you must be Father Stevens. Very nice to meet you."

"Likewise. I hear you're headed to Salem. I've spent some time up there."

"Yes, I have some family there so when a position opened up, I decided to make the move. I'll miss my girls, though."

"I can imagine."

"I wish I could take them with me, you know? Girls are very impressionable at this age. Oh, some will put on a brave front, act tough and all. Most of them are good kids."

"Most of them?"

"Well, I shouldn't say anything, but Father Halloran has a secret program. To help some of the kids who are considered 'at-risk'."

"Really? That's very charitable."

"Yes, Father Halloran seeks out these girls since many of them come from poor backgrounds. Not all, but some."

"Interesting. I have to ask him about that."

"Yes, I'm sure he'd like the help."

"So, what's today's lesson?"

"We've been studying some local authors. We started with some American classics at the beginning of the school year. Today we are discussing The Scarlet Letter. Hawthorne really wrote a barnburner with this one!"

"It's a classic!"

Jack began to notice a theme. Halloran's fire and brimstone speech and now a classic story about adultery. He didn't like where this was going. "Father Malone,"

"Mitch, please. I miss hearing my first name."

"Okay, Mitch. Who chooses the curriculum here?"

"Typically, we all put in requests for certain books or specific subject focus items, but Father Halloran has the final say. He has a favorite stash in the closet next to his office. The Father loves classic American Literature as do I, but I was hoping to do more science fiction. He said maybe, but that it would be difficult to hold the students' attention. 'Girl respond to romantic stories; boys like the adventure and science fiction stories, so The Scarlet Letter it is."

Just then, the ancient public address system crackled to life. "MARTHA BENSON, REPORT TO THE SCHOOL ADMINISTRATOR'S OFFICE, MARTHA BENSON TO THE ADMINISTRATOR'S OFFICE."

Jack was beginning to see an uncomfortable trend.

Jack left Father Malone's classroom and headed to the teacher's lounge for a coffee. He passed the nurse's office and saw another girl sitting on the examination bench. She held herself the same way the other girl he saw did. Jack found it a little disturbing but he couldn't put his finger on it. He walked in to talk to the nurse but she wasn't there. "Excuse me, young lady," Jack was trying to use his most priest-like voice. "Where is the nurse?"

"Sister Rose isn't here." The girl was not in a talking mood.

"Will she be back soon?"

"I don't know." The girl got up and left in a hurry. Jack was getting that old feeling again, when he knew there were things happening below the surface. He decided he'd get his coffee and plan his next move.

The lounge was buzzing with activity. Jack saw Father Malone at a table with two other women. From what he had heard, nuns weren't required to wear their traditional habits; a few of the older nuns did but most didn't. The younger nuns felt it was easier to relate to the students. There was a definite age gap with the staff. Jack had sat down with his coffee when Father Halloran came in. The temperature of the room immediately dropped and the happy chatter stopped abruptly. "Good Morning, All." Halloran seemed to like the effect he had on the staff. He looked over and saw Jack alone. "Can I get everyone's attention, please! We have here with us a new teacher on staff today. Would you all greet Father Philip Stevens, Father Malone's replacement." Weak clapping and a murmur followed. Undaunted, Father Halloran continued. "As you all know, Father Malone has been asked to take over St. Anne's Parish in Salem, Mass. He will also have his hands full as the Campus Catholic Liaison for Salem State University. I don't know which is harder, high school students or college kids!" Halloran laughed at his own joke. The longer Jack observed Halloran, the less he liked him and he didn't like him from the start. "Thank you!" Halloran came over to the table and the ladies excused themselves. Jack stood up and Halloran waved him back down. "No need to be formal, Philip. Nice to have you on board. Since you came early,

I'd like to invite you to next college mixer. We have them to encourage our young ladies to consider college once they left us. The next one is after school on this Friday at the rectory on Chestnut St."

Using a practiced stammer, Jack replied, "S-s-sure, Father. I'd be happy to. Should I bring anything?"

"No, just bring your experience. The girls will have questions."

The invitation rang in Jack's head as he walked back towards the class-room. He was disgusted but at the same time he knew he couldn't refuse Halloran's offer. He had to get to know the situation and figure out if Halloran was Shackelton's supplier or vice versa. As Jack was pondering his next move, he found himself passing the nurse's office. He expected to see a student sitting next to the desk, but instead he saw a nun in full habit. She was older, early sixties, about five foot three. She had a medical pin on her left breast and young hands. Jack decided to introduce himself. "Hello, I'm Father Stevens." The woman looked up and said, Good Morning, Father. My name is Sister Rose. You can call me that or Nurse Rose. Welcome to St. Baskins." Her attitude was pleasant but guarded.

"I've noticed several girls in here recently, I was wondering if some-thing is going around."

"Just puberty, Father. Teenage girls' bodies are blooming every day. Sometimes they just need a place to suffer. I have an open-door policy so many of them come in to be alone for a time. Some need some phar-maceutical relief, while other need a sympathetic ear."

"That's a great policy. I'm sure you've helped a lot of young ladies."

"I try."

Jack chose his next words carefully. "Have any of them come to you with other issues?"

Sister Rose raised an eyebrow. "Like what?"

"Specifically, abuse. You see, in the past I've worked with some at-risk students and I would be willing to-"

"That won't be necessary, Father." Sister Rose's tone became tight. "If you will excuse me, I have much work to do."

"Of course. Good day." It didn't take a seasoned detective to see that Sister Rose was hiding something. She knew more than she let on and Jack was going to have to find out what it was.

The rest of the day was uneventful. Jack was eager to get home and continue going through Detective Brown's files. As Jack was getting into his car, he noticed Father Halloran talking to a student. He was stroking her hair as if he was dating her; behavior that would be particularly inappropriate for any school official. Once they were done speaking, she walked away holding herself in the now familiar 'basket' style Jack had seen in the nurse's office. Jack hesitated long enough to see Halloran turn and walk back towards the school. The girl picked up her school bag near a tree and started walking down the driveway. Jack pulled up several yards in front of the girl and stopped. He watched her in the rearview mirror until she got close but not too close. He got out of his car and called to the girl. "Excuse me! Young lady!" The girl froze with a look of abject terror on her face. "Y-yes?"

Jack saw the look and tried to put her at ease. "I'm sorry to trouble you but my phone isn't working. I need to make a call would you have one I can borrow?"

"Phones aren't allowed at school. It's at home."

"Oh, that's right! I'm new here, I'm Father Stevens." Jack held his hand out. The girl hesitated and then shook it weakly. "My name is Shannon Doherty."

"It's nice to meet you, Shannon. You know, I believe I saw you talking to Father Halloran a few minutes ago." Jack changed his tone to a more serious one. "Are you okay?"

Shannon nodded. "Yes."

"Well, if you ever need someone to talk to, I'm a friendly ear."

Shannon produced a weak smile. "Thanks. I have to get home."

"Okay. I'd offer a ride but I believe it's against school policy."

"No one ever follows that."

"Well, since I'm new, I should uphold the rules for now. Be safe getting home, okay?"

"Okay."

Jack immediately got into his car and pulled out. He watched Shannon for a time but didn't linger. She was nervous and uncomfortable and Father Halloran made her that way. Jack thought about things on the drive home. Route 2 can be hairy heading west. It's a strange highway with traffic lights one moment then an expressway the next. Jack didn't mind since school got out before rush hour. He pulled in his driveway 47 minutes later and parked. Alma was napping on the living room couch. Jack walked in and saw her. He kissed her on the forehead and quietly went into the bedroom to change. He grabbed a ginger ale from the fridge and brought it into the den. He pulled out his laptop and the case files for Atwell and Janice Marston. He plugged in the thumb drive and picked up where he left off the night before. Since he came straight home, he had more time to review the files. He opened the folder, 'Janice Marston':

Janice Marston

Janice Helen Marston (born June 12, 1994; disappeared December 11, 2019), also known as Janice Marston, was a 25-year-old American office worker from Burlington, Mass who was employed at a computer manufacturer. She disappeared on December 11, 2019. Her body was discovered on December 13, 2019 at the Hobbs Brook Reservoir, two days after her disappearance. Her murder remains unsolved.

Biography

Janice Helen Marston was born on June 12, 1999 in Salem, New Hampshire to Claude Marston, Sr (1939–2010) and Darlene Martha (nee Dixon) Marston (b. 1954). She had three brothers, Ronald Philip Marston (1974–2018), Darrin Marston, Matthew Marston. Marston was living in the Holmes Village section of Burlington, MA and worked as an administrative assistant at the Waters Corporation, Bedford, MA.

On December 11, 2019, Marston went Christmas shopping at the Arsenal Mall, in Watertown. She was wearing a green turtleneck sweater and leather skirt, and was scheduled to meet a boyfriend stationed at Hanscom Air Force Base for a date, but never appeared. Her disappearance occurred seven days after the disappearance of Mary Atwell. The two women looked remarkably similar. Two days later, Marston's body was discovered partially in the water and partially on the banks of Hobbs Brook Reservoir, by two park rangers working with a survey team. She was found with her hands tied behind her back, and with scratches and bruises on her body, indicating she had struggled with her assailant. An autopsy performed by Dr. Walter Maharis indicated the cause of death was a single deep knife wound found in Marston's throat. She had approximately "15 superficial cuts on the neck and abrasions on her forehead, nose and chin". She had gun powder residue in her mouth with similar abrasions as Atwell, with teeth missing as well.

Disappearance and death

Marston's body was found on federal property, and the case was therefore under FBI jurisdiction. At the time, FBI agents believed there was a possible link with the disappearance of Mary Atwell: both women had been shopping in close proximity, had similar builds, and disappeared within days of each other. However, the FBI was unable to link the two cases. Thomas A. Reagan, special FBI agent in charge of the Boston office, claimed to have a number of suspects. The FBI remains the lead agency for this case, and despite information circulating online, the investigation has not been handed over to the Massachusetts State Police Department, nor local police.

In early 2020, Pamela Croton and Jennifer Stone, two alleged victims who suffered sexual abuse at St. Baskins High School at the hands of Father Joseph Halloran, came forward filing charges against the Roman Catholic Archdiocese of Boston. Croton claimed to the Watertown police that Halloran had shown her Atwell's body. Consequently, Middlesex County police reopened Atwell's case and reviewed a possible connection with Marston's. The police received numerous telephone calls providing information regarding Atwell's murder after local news reports about the allegations against Halloran renewed public interest. It was discovered that Marston had spent time around Halloran.

Since the Atwell and Marston's murders, two additional murders have occurred in the area. On January 16, 2020, 16-year-old Lynn Deroliers also disappeared from the Assembly Square Mall. Deroliers' body was discovered on January 20, 2020 in Cambridge, between the eastbound and westbound lanes of Storrow Drive, after a snow plow driver spotted the body.

On April 27, 2020, 16-year-old Xioxian Xhan, female, of the Nottingham, White and Bell School disappeared from Fresh Pond Shopping center. Her body was found two days later in the Mount Auburn Cemetery in Cambridge. DNA tests were inconclusive.

Jack was puzzled. "Inconclusive?", he thought. "This area has some of the best DNA labs in the country. How could they have not found any DNA?" The coroner's report seemed to answer that question:

COMMONWEALTH OF MASSACHUSETTS

Office of the Chief Medical Examiner Headquarters

Boston Medical Center

720 Albany St.,

Boston, MA 02118

ON SITE SUMMARY

DECEASED: Janice Marston

The patient was a 25-year-old Caucasian female with no significant past medical history. The patient's body was found partially submerged in the waters of the Hobbs Brook Reservoir. The patient had been found by a park ranger at 9:30 am on December 15, 2019. Upon the coroner's arrival, it observed that the body was partially submerged in the water. There were lacerations to the head and neck, with a large gash, severing the carotid artery. There was no blood around the body and analysis of the sand underneath the body resulted in no traces of blood which would establish the fact that the victim had been murdered somewhere else.

FULL AUTOPSY REPORT

The victim's body was fully intact with no missing parts. Hair was filled with sand and dirt. She suffered a severe blow to the back of the head which would have rendered her unconscious. Her clothes were intact, with the exception of her skirt which had been partially lowered below her hips. There is no evidence of sexual assault, but skin and hair had been found underneath her fingernails, along with the lacerations on her face and neck suggests that she struggled with her attacker. DNA test results were inconclusive due to the DNA being not on file with the Combined DNA Index System (CODIS).

DESCRIPTION OF GROSS LESIONS:

EXTERNAL EXAMINATION: The body is that of a 25-year-old well developed, well-nourished white female. There is no peripheral edema of the extremities. There is an area of bruising on the upper chest and anterior neck. There are multiple small areas of hemorrhage bilaterally in the conjunctiva. A severe laceration is apparent on the right side of the face along with some bruising and gouge. It appears the victim was struck in the face with a coarse object. The patient has no other major surgical scars.

TOXICOLOGY

There were no foreign materials in the stomach. There was a small amount of undigested food and soda in the victim's stomach. Her blood was clear of any type of drug or alcohol.

Jack noticed that the report went on further. He thought it would be better to review more about Halloran. He clicked on the Halloran folder. A file named 'Vital Stats' caught his attention. Jack opened it and found a document that read like a resume:

SUBJECT: Alfred Joseph Halloran

AGE: 47

HAIR: Salt and pepper, normal kept short in almost military fashion.

EYES: Brown, wears corrective lenses

HEIGHT: 6'0"

Birthplace: Solomon Village, Newark, NJ

GENERAL DESCRIPTION: Medium build, normal weight to height ratio. Typically, seen clean shaven, presents himself as a member of the Catholic clergy. Subject has questionable record with Archdiocese of Boston with respect to suspected sexual abuse with minors in the church. Nothing has been reported to law enforcement but internal sources from the Archdiocese suggest that Halloran has engaged in sexual abuse and cover ups.

Early life: Little is known about Halloran's family life and childhood. Records indicate that he graduated from Colodny Catholic High School in 1989, located in the Solomon Village section of Newark, New Jersey. He then attended St. Anthony's Seminary and College in Bradentown, Long Island, NY.

Work History: Halloran seems to move around about every three years. Since his graduation from seminary in 1994, he served as associate pastor at St. Amelia's Parish in Teaneck, Our Lady of Redemption in Princeton, and The Brotherhood of St. Vincent in Mamoroneck. He was also the prison chaplain at Ingleside Correctional Facility, Beechmont Falls, New Jersey.

As of September of 2015, he is the Headmaster at St. Baskins Preparatory School in Watertown, MA. Sources revealed that he has been engaging in possible abusive behavior. Other sources suggest he may be involved in human trafficking.

Jack felt his blood pressure go up. "I really don't like this guy", he thought to himself. The words 'human trafficking' steeled his resolve to put Halloran away. The one thing that bothered him was the connection to Shackelton. There had to be more incentive for him to move from New Jersey to Boston. Jack looked up Shackelton's file and saw that he had attended college but didn't finish. The name of the college was not found in the file. He thought for a moment and pulled out Agent Stanton's card. He called him and Stanton picked up on the second ring. "Hello?"

"Agent Stanton, Jack Chase."

"How are things going?"

"Slow, but I need some information."

"If I can, sure."

"The files you gave me said that Shackelton went to college but it doesn't say where. Can you find out?"

"I think so. That's a pretty specific request. Sounds like a hunch."
"That's exactly what it is. If I can confirm it, we may have our connection for these two that go beyond priest and parishioner."

"I'll put in the request immediately."

"Thanks. Call me anytime when you get it."

"Certainly."

Jack hung up and heard someone in the kitchen. He figured it was Alma so he decided to take a break. Alma was heating up some leftovers. "Oh! There you are. I thought I'd fix you a quick bite."

"That's great. Thank you."

"How is Father Stevens today?"

"He's ready to strangle this guy Halloran. Everything says he's dirty, I just have to prove it."

"Do you think you can?"

"Not sure. I have a feeling I may need to catch him in the act."

"Sounds like you a hidden camera."

"Not a bad idea."

Alma smiled. "I have them occasionally."

"Oh, more than occasionally."

"You charmer!" Alma planted a kiss on Jack's lips. "Anyway, I have to go this thing Halloran does with the students."

"Do you think he uses that to get the girls?"

"I think it's part of it. I still haven't put the pieces together." Jack looked at the clock. "What time does Best Buy close?"

"Not sure. Ten, I think."

"Wanna go for a ride?"

"Eat your dinner first." Jack smiled and sat down at the table.

Jack arrived at St. Baskins early Friday morning. He walked into the school and right into the office. "Good Morning, Moira."

Moira was her usual cheery self. "Good Morning, Father."

"Father Halloran has asked me to attend the mixer after school. I believe he said it was at the Rectory?"

All of the color drained from Moira's face. "Sure, I'll print up some directions."

Jack noticed Moira's attitude change for a moment. "Is there something wrong?"

"No! Not at all! It's just that-"

"What?"

"A lot of the faculty are not fans of the mixers. Father Halloran insists they are a good way to prepare our students but many of the students feel that they favor some over others. If this were a public school, they couldn't have them but Father Halloran has a firm control over the school board."

"I see. Well, I told him I would go so I will see if there is something I can do."

"Thank you, Father. Good luck."

Jack was beginning to feel like these mixers were the key, but there was still no connection between Halloran, Shackelton and the students. He continued his day without any incident. He audited Father Malone's English class and made arrangements to take over on Monday. As the last class of the day ended, he made his way towards the office. He passed the nurse's office and he noticed that the door was shut. He heard voices, one male and one female. The door was solid wood so Jack strained to listen. It wasn't an argument but it was definitely a spirited conversation. Once they stopped, he walked quickly towards the office. By the time he got to the office he innocently turned to look at the nurse's door. Father Halloran emerged and turned toward his office. Jack decided he'd better enlist some technology to help him figure out what is happening. He thought that while Halloran was at the mixer, he'd plant a small, hidden camera with a microphone in his office. Jack entered the office and Moira was on the phone. Jack checked his bag and made sure his Best Buy purchase was out of the package. Moira hung up the phone. "Excuse me, Moira. I'd like to see what books are available for my English class for next week. Where would I find the storage closet Father Malone used?"

"Oh, he usually gets them from Father Halloran but you can browse the storage closet. It's next to his office. Here, if you want to look at the books he has in there, here are the keys."

"Thank you. I'll bring these back shortly."

"Thanks, Father. I have some work to finish up but I'd like to be out by 3:30."

Jack looked at the clock. It was 2:50. "No problem, I'll just take a quick peek."

Moira smiled but Jack remembered her reaction to the his attending the mixer. He knew he may not get a second chance to bug Halloran's office. He jogged a bit down to Halloran's office. Jack had been a teacher long enough to know since the school building had been built in the 1950s, the locks and door hardware lasts forever. That usually meant that the keys to a closet may also open an adjacent office or another closet. Jack tried the key on Halloran's door but no success. He thought that there might be a connecting door from the closet to the office and his hunch paid off. He got into the closet and turned the light on. Jack closed the door and glanced at the books to make sure he actually had material for next week. He took a copy of 'Of Mice and Men' and then searched the rest of the closet. Behind some dusty books was a metal chest that did not have any dust on it. "Strange." Jack thought. The chest was unlocked so Jack opened it. What he found was pornography so racy, it would make a Marine blush. He also found thumb drives, rewritable DVDs, CDs and a journal. Jack figured it belonged to Halloran so he put everything back, planning to come back and copy it all. He also found the door to Halloran's office. He put his hand on the knob and heard someone come in. Jack froze and listened through the door. He heard Halloran with someone else in the office. "I just need to grab a few things. Come in and close the door." Sound of a door shutting. "You want a drink?"

The other man said, "Are you kidding? Pour away!"

"I love these things. The bookcase looks so academic. No one would suspect I have a full bar built into it. I got the idea when I saw a YouTube video about a company that make secret gun rack and those secret panic rooms. I found some designs on the Dark Web and built it myself."

"You're pretty freaking handy for a priest."

"I'm a man first. That's one of the perks here. I make those little bitches do what I want and when I want."

"What about the nuns?"

"The nuns know I can destroy them if I wanted. I had a run in with Rita."

"Let me guess. She was whining about protecting the girls and helping them and all that crap."

"Yep. Then I reminded her that her retirement fund could suffer a serious blow if she screwed things up."

"So, what about this new guy?"

"I invited him to the mixer today. We'll size him up and see if is up for membership."

"Joe, what if this guy is solid? I mean most of the priests don't even know about the operation."

"That's why I invited him to the mixer. Today, no fooling around. The guys play it straight and we test him out. If he comes on board, then we'll use him. If not, then he's just filler, like Malone."

"Does Malone know anything?"

"No. I think he may have suspected so pulled a few strings to get him out of here. About half the faculty are on board, the other half has no clue."

"Man, if you were in business, you'd be armpit deep in cash!" The man laughed.

Halloran laughed, too. "What make you think I'm not in business? Becoming a priest was best financial move I've ever made! You should see the kind of money the Archdiocese brings in on contributions alone! Plus, this side venture turned out better than I could have dreamed."

"I had no idea. I mean, my mother always wanted me to be a priest."

"Mine, too. So much so that she beat me every day until I out grew her. Then I was one giving the beatings. But at that point I figured it was easy work and I learned that everybody loves a priest."

"You got that right. I can drive as fast as I want and if I get pulled over and I'm wearing this thing, the cop lets me off. It's the best get out of jail card you can get! And even if the guy gives me a ticket, one phone call and it disappears."

Both men chuckled. Jack heard the sound of a drawer opening. "Most importantly though, I keep the files hidden. I have a box in the closet."

"Hey, it's almost time. We should go."

"All right. I can put it away on Monday. Nobody'll be in here."

"Hey, what about Shackelton? How long do you think he'll serve?"

"Don't know. I've got friends in the DA's office so I'll turn on the priestly charm and see what they'll do. Personally, I should let him rot for being careless. He never should have gone to a small town. I told him, big cities, high populations. Good yield and it's harder to find missing girls."

"Hiding in plain sight. Good advice."

"Neil, I am an expert in hiding in plain sight. It's effective and easy! Let's go."

The two men left and Jack's heart started beating again. His suspicions confirmed, he wasted no time in getting into Halloran's office. He didn't have much time before the mixer so he planted the cameras in strategic placed and tested them on his cell phone. He made sure that they would upload automatically to his private Google account. "Thanks, Courtney," he thought. Jack decided to examine the bookcase before he left. He felt around the shelves and discovered the middle shelf of books were phony. He tugged at all of them until the second to last one. The bookcase clicked and swung open. Jack inspected the contents and found some very old wine, 50-year-old single malt scotch and other expensive liquor. He found some files, some dirty magazines, and seven pictures of female students. They were taken in the office and the girls did not look happy. Jack took out his cell phone and took pictures of the pictures and put them back. He looked up on the top shelf above the bar and found a fairly expensive digital camera that was set behind an angled hole through the bookcase. It was set to film anyone sitting opposite Halloran at his desk. Jack made a mental note of that and quickly checked the pictures he took as he closed up the bookcase. He checked the doors to the closet and Halloran's office to make sure they were closed and locked. Jack began to walk away, but then he thought better and wiped the door knobs off. He went back to the office to return the keys but Moira had already left. His bag was on the floor in front of the door. She taped a note to the office door:

Father Stevens,

Sorry I couldn't wait for you. Just bring the keys back to school on Monday.

Have a Great Weekend! Moira

"Perfect!" Jack thought. He grabbed his bag and immediately went out to his car. He looked up the nearest locksmith to his home and put the address in his phone. He drove immediately to the rectory.

The rectory was an attractive New England style colonial farmhouse. It had a large entryway with a wrap-around porch and classic columns. The front door was a large, extra wide entrance, painted white like the rest of the exterior. Jack noticed the antiseptic nature of the place, much like a funeral home. He went into the front and a group of men was standing there. Most had their backs to the door and several turned around as Jack walked in. The first one was Halloran. "Philip! How are you! Glad you could make it! Let me introduce you the others." He turned Jack to a hatchet-faced man. "This is Father Neil McHenry. He's a math teacher so you guys may not cross paths very much." Jack shook the hand of the man he heard in Halloran's office. He had dark hair with a 1950's crew cut, wire rim glasses and a slender build. "Nice to meet you."

"We're all on a first name basis here, well the men are. This is Bill Wachovick from Sister Amelia Junior College, up in Brookdale, New Hampshire. This is Bob Taylor from Ablehurst in Putnam, Connecticut, and this is Tom Reasoner from The Trivellium School in Bolton, Mass. Gentlemen, this is Philip Stevens. He comes highly recommended from Greenfield Catholic out west. Welcome. There are refreshments in the dining room and the girls are waiting for us in the parlor."

Jack felt a darkness he's never felt before. He didn't have much of an appetite, but he perused the refreshments as if he did. He needed to figure out how to pin down Halloran and anyone else involved. Jack moved into the parlor. There were about twelve girls seated in the parlor. They were wearing minimal make up and dressed in nondescript, business-like suits. There was a lectern at the front of the parlor and Halloran was standing at it. The other men filtered in with Jack. Halloran looked around and once everyone had settled in, he began. "Welcome, ladies! This is the final College Mixer of the year. You are all graduating in a couple of months and we at St. Baskins want to make sure you have a smooth transition. So, we have asked some of our college liaison officers from several catholic colleges to come and visit us here in this informal venue. For the next two hours, we will rotate you through a series of interviews, don't worry these are for practice for when you do them after graduation. The following students will go with Mr. Taylor." Halloran read list of names and the girls stood up and exited the room with Taylor. "The next group will go with Mr. Wachovick." Same routine with each group being about ten girls. The last group went with Halloran and Tom Reasoner. "Hey Philip! Come with us." Halloran was more like a game show host than a priest preparing young girls for college. "Now this is simple. We give them a pep talk. We keep it balanced. We tell them that they can go to college to start a career or to meet a husband. We'll prepare them either way." Everything Halloran said to Jack carried an ominous tone. Jack felt a nervous tightening in his gut. He followed Halloran and Reasoner into a room upstairs about half the size of the parlor. "Have a seat, ladies." The girls came in and sat down. "We have a treat for you today. Our new English teacher, Father Stevens is joining us today. Now, many of you may have heard about these mixers but today you'll get a firsthand experience." Halloran went on about the benefits of college and 'good' Catholic women have a good work life balance. It would have been a great speech, if Halloran wasn't such a snake. Finally, he concluded. "So now you can enjoy the refreshments downstairs and wait for your personal meeting." The girls crossed themselves and began to exit the room. Jack was standing near the door when Halloran stopped one particular girl. She had long straight black hair. "Martha Benson. You will meet with Father McHenry. We have some things to discuss with you." Jack watched her as a look of abject fear came over her face. He began to follow them as they went down the hall. Halloran called him back. "Philip! You can stay with me. We're staying in this room."

"Right, okay. I was wondering what Father McHenry was going to talk to Martha about."

Halloran smiled a phony smile. "Martha needs some discipline. She was the one who posted those pictures of Father Blake and Sister Elise on the school site."

"Right so she is a Senior?"

"No, most of these girls are Juniors. We want them to spend their Senior year preparing for college while finishing their studies. We have them continue to attend the mixers throughout their Senior year. So, actually, if you could come in and just talk about your college experience to the girls, that would be a great help."

Jack was concerned about the discipline Martha was going to receive at Halloran's hand. McHenry had an obvious, 'holier than thou' attitude and didn't try to hide it. "These youngsters need a firm hand these days. Their parents spoil them until they can't control them anymore."

"That seems to the be the general feeling." Jack was trying to keep his cool.

"We at St. Baskins are very 'old school' pun intended!" McHenry's laugh was hollow.

"I've been successful at keeping a balance. My students have responded well when I combined discipline with encouragement."

"Ha. You are one of those new thinkers, eh? Talk to the kids rather than hard, strict, corporal punishment."

"I would never lay a finger on a student. I believe in being strict, but it has to be tempered. Otherwise, it can easily cross over into abuse."

McHenry's smile faded. "Philip, we need to get back to basics! Our entire society is on the brink of disaster. Boys are becoming more effeminate! They engage in unnatural acts at an alarmingly young age! If we don't train the females to retake and retain their roles in society, our country, our world will come apart!"

"What do you suggest we do about that?"

"Turn the clock back. Have women go back to being the submissive, obedient creatures they were intended to be."

"So, why offer them help for college?"

"They should still go to college, primarily to meet a husband. That's why we only recommend schools that share our philosophy."

"I see. What types of things do you say to them? I mean, I have to believe not all of them will want to just settle down."

"Remedial training. That's what Martha Benson is going through now. She had been rebellious through most of her schooling. Finally, today she will get the kind of direction she lacked for so long."

Jack was very scared for Martha. McHenry's veiled explanation of what was going to happen to her chilled him to the bone. "Excuse me, where's the bathroom?"

McHenry pointed. "Down the hall, on the right. Are you okay?"

"Had some of the chicken curry for lunch at the cafeteria. I don't think it's sitting well."

"That happened to me once." McHenry leaned in close. "I never eat school food, it's terrible!" He laughed as Jack smiled and dashed off. He did have to go to the bathroom but he needed to be out of sight until he could find Martha Benson. Jack checked several rooms until he heard Halloran's voice. It was low and menacing.

"I cannot tell you how disappointed I am in you, Martha. I thought we had worked through these issues."

"You can't scare me anymore. I've told my parents about what you and McHenry have to me. To all of us. We also know that you killed Sister Mary!"

"Oh, dear child! You are confused. But a morality session will help you."

"I'm not stupid! You just want to get your hands on me!" Jack knew he had to act. Halloran's voice got harsher. "Martha, you really need to get a handle on things, you must,-"

Jack pounded on the door. "Father Halloran! Father Halloran!"

Halloran whipped the door open angrily, "What do you want?" Jack faked a jump scare. "I-I'm sorry to interrupt but there's an urgent call for you downstairs in the kitchen!"

"Hmmuph. Excuse me, Philip. Martha, I will be back." Halloran stomped down the hall towards the back stairs. Jack acted quickly. "Come on!"

Martha was shocked. "What are going to do with me?"

"Get you out of here and away from him! Let's go!"

Jack grabbed Martha's hand and they bounded down the front stairs. They ran to Jack's car and jumped in. Jack tore out of the parking lot and drove down the street. Martha looked around and put her face in her hands and burst into tears. Jack took a breath and realized Martha was crying. He pulled into a Dunkin Donuts and stopped. "Are you okay?"

Martha took a moment and said, "Yes. Thank you."

"Is this the first time he's tried to rape you?"

Martha looked at Jack in shock. "No. He's done it to me so many times, I've lost count."

"When did start doing things to you?"

"Ninth grade. Right when he first got there. Him and McHenry."

"McHenry's raped you, too?"

"Sometimes they do it together. Especially at these mixers. Half the time they're getting us drunk so we don't know what's going on, the other half, when there are new girls or new men, they'll play it straight."

"I suspect Halloran was mad at you for posting the picture of Blake on the website."

"It was the only way I could get anyone's attention. No one at the school is willing to help us. Our parents don't believe us and when they do, Halloran denies it and says we're the problem."

"Listen, I am here to help you and the other girls. Do you have proof that Halloran had Sister Mary Atwell killed?"

"Yes. We snuck our cell phones in for a while when Sister Mary disappeared. We would have gone to the police but Halloran is the police chaplain so we kept it as insurance."

"Who is 'we'? Have other girls been abused?"

"Yes, we have a list, dates, and detail hidden away."

"Can you get them? We will need them to take Halloran down."

"How can I be sure? How can I trust you?"

"I can't tell you why, not yet. But you can trust me and you'll know why eventually. Right now, I am going to bring you home and I want you to stay there. Tell your parents that the FBI is involved but you know nothing else."

Martha's face brightened up. "The FBI? Gosh, I hope you can really help us."

"I will."

Jack dropped off Martha and headed back to the school. It was after seven so no one should be there. He knew had to retrieve the contents of that metal box he found in Halloran's closet. The FBI supplied him with a laptop with an external hard drive and special software that performs high speed downloads. Jack kept it in the trunk of his rental car just in case of such situations. Jack pulled around the back of the school opened the trunk. He decided to park his car in the patch of woods next to the school in case someone came through the area. At the moment, no one was around and it was twilight. He got out the laptop and readied the keys. He wanted to get in and copy the files as soon as possible. Jack got in quickly and found the metal box. He got them downloaded and thought to check the camera footage but he decided to do it when he got home. Jack's heartbeat was loud in his ears as he moved quickly out his car. He saw another car pull through the lot slowly and continue through driveway. He held still and waited for it to pass by. Once Jack thought the coast was clear he started his car and drove home. Once he got onto Route 2, he called Stanton. "I just rescued a student from Halloran."

"What? What do you mean?"

"I'll get into that later. I need someone to protect a student named Martha Benson. Lives in Waverley, address is 20 Gardenfield Road."

"Done."

"Oh, and keep it discreet if you would."

"You didn't blow your cover, did you?"

"I don't think so. I've copied some files I found and they may blow this thing wide open."

"Let's meet on Monday."

"Better make it Sunday morning. Father Philip will be at mass but Jack Chase should be free."

"Sunday it is. Meet me in Westford. I'll text you the address. 11am."

"See you then."

Jack breathed easier once he got into Concord. He had mixed feelings about what would be in Halloran's secret files. It's rare to find such damning evidence this early in an investigation. Jack hadn't been at the school a full week. He realized that Halloran, McHenry and others would have to have a high level of hubris to believe that they could get away with this kind of abuse. The lack of any kind security at the school, the old school locks and the blind trust would certainly cause some type of calamity at some point; or rather allow the abuse of power and control. Jack was itching to see what was in those files.

It was 8:35pm when Jack pulled into his yard. He was glad to be home and Alma was happy to see him. They sat down to a late supper and Jack filled her in on the day's adventure. "You have to be kidding me! That poor girl!"

"She not the only one. I only hope I can talk my way out of it on Monday. In the meantime, I need to find out what's in those files."

"Well, it sounds like a late night, so I will leave you to it. Leave the dishes, I'll pick up."

"Thanks, Hun. You are a life saver."

"Are you telling me I'm sweet as candy?"

"More than that. I couldn't do this without your help. Thanks."

"My pleasure, Sweetie."

Jack hugged Alma for a long time and kissed her. For a moment he thought he'd ask her to marry him but he felt he should finish the case first. He wanted to do it right and he was willing to pick the right moment. Jack remembered how anxious he was to see was on Halloran's private files. He took out his laptop and the special external drive and fired it up. There were about three dozen files all with girls' names. Jack hesitated opening the first one, a sense of dread seeping into his gut about what he would find. Nevertheless, he pressed on. The first folder was called Theresa Delvecchio. It had several jpeg pictures, some sound files and some video. He sorted them by their date created and opened the oldest one. It was dated January 21, 2017. It was a photograph of a young girl, dressed in a St. Baskins' school uniform. She was holding a card with her name on it. She looked about fourteen years old. Jack took out a pad of paper and copied her name down. He opened the next jpeg and it was the same girl, but dressed up as if she were going to prom. The next photograph Theresa was dressed very provocatively, heavy make-up and high heels. She had a profoundly sad expression on her face. Several of the following photographs showed poor Theresa in very adult situations involving nudity and pornographic situations. Jack continued through several of the files and it was the same modus operandi for about twenty girls. Jack looked at a few of the videos and found more of the same. Several of them started off with the girl pleading for them to stop. Then reservation and then obedience. It was if something died in the girls and they lost the will to fight back. Some were beaten others were tied up and put into another room. It was terrible. Jack began to tear up. He couldn't contain his anger but grieved for the loss of innocence of these girls. Finally, he opened a folder called SisterA. In it were several videos that appeared to be shot in Halloran's office. Jack checked the length of the first video and it was about three minutes long. It started with a shot of Halloran's office, the chair on the opposite side of his desk. After about 20 seconds, a nun comes in and sits in the chair. Jack felt his blood run cold as he realized it was Mary Atwell.

Atwell: You wanted to see me, Father?

Halloran: Yes, Sister Mary. You see there have been rumors going around that some of the students have been engaging in sinful behaviors of the flesh or accusing faculty of it.

Atwell: I haven't heard anything.

Halloran: Come now, Sister. It's no secret that many of the girls confide in you. You are young, really not too much older than them. Certainly, someone has told you something?

Atwell: I am sorry father, no.

Halloran: That's unfortunate. Father McHenry, have you heard anything?

McHenry (off camera): It is too sordid to repeat, Father Halloran.

Halloran: Oh, do try, Father.

McHenry: It's seems that some of it was directed at the two of us!"

Atwell: Oh, that's terrible. Is there a particular girl you need me to talk to?

Halloran: Not right now, Sister. We will let you know. And you need to tell us if any one says more of these terrible things, do I make myself clear?

Atwell: Of course, Father.

Halloran: Thank you. That is all.

Jack clicked on the next video clip. Same setting but Mary Atwell was already seated at Halloran's desk. She was much more animated this time:

Atwell: Father, you must know that several of the girls complained of the same thing!

Halloran: Sister, these are the musings of silly school girls! They are going through puberty and they say stupid things.

Atwell: I have talked to eleven girls through all the grades, each one saying that you and Father McHenry were touching them! How can I ignore that?

Halloran: You will ignore the stupid lies of these stupid girls! You are to speak to no one about anything they said!

Atwell: Tell me it's not true!

Halloran: What?

Atwell: Tell me it isn't true! I did some checking. You've only been here for eighteen months and before that you were only at your last parish for three years and the same before that. The Archdiocese only moves people that much when there's a problem.

Halloran: My dear Sister, I only go where the Lord directs me. I moved because the Cardinal needed me to fix some problems, that's all! Now we need to work as a team. I have not done anything that endanger or hurt these girls. You must believe that.

Jack noticed that Halloran discreetly opened his desk drawer and took out what looked like a revolver.

Halloran: Sister, why don't you meet me at the rectory. I will show you the counseling forms that the girls signed and the videos of those sessions. That will show you that I have done nothing inappropriate.

Atwell: I will meet you at 7:30 tonight. I have to run home and then a few errands to do.

Halloran: Perfect.

Atwell gets up and leaves the office. Jack notices there's another minute and a half to the video. After almost a full minute of Halloran sitting at his desk, he finally makes a phone call.

Halloran: Get up here, now.

Unheard response.

Halloran: Okay, fine. Atwell has become a problem. I suspected she might go this far.

Unheard response.

Halloran: You take her away and do it. Make sure there's no connection.

Unheard response.

Halloran: I'll send McHenry with you. She's a woman, you three should be able to handle it. Let me know when it's done.

Jack had the evidence. The problem is that since Jack found it without a warrant he didn't know if it would be admissible in court. He set that aside in his mind and continued going through the files. It was almost 9:30. Jack found a folder called, 'Finances'. He clicked on it and there were several spreadsheets with names, dates and dollar amounts. Jack printed it off and suspected these were Halloran's customers. "He cagey. He doesn't trust anyone," Jack thought. There was a video file in the same folder. Thinking it odd, Jack opened it. It started as the others did. It was a shot of Halloran's office, the opposite chair. There were some background noises then Halloran appeared with a drink, probably from his secret bar. He sat in the chair facing his desk and addressed the camera:

Halloran: I am making this video in case something happens to me. It's unlikely of course but they say you can never be too careful. I guess I don't know where to start. I got into the priesthood because that's what I was supposed to do. I thought about doing other things but then I discovered I had great power and influence as a priest. I never had that growing up. Scrawny kid from Long Island. Anyway, included with this video is a list of all the men who were customers. Influential men, who at their request, and at great expense and risk, wanted these young girls. Should anything happen to me, there is video, saved to a disk labeled, 'Services Rendered'. I don't expect to ever have to use it as leverage but you never know. I have a lawyer, also a customer, who has explicit instructions to release this to the press if anything should happen to me. His is the only name left off the list as payment for holding the information contained in the disk. I have copies hidden and so does he.

Halloran gets up out of the chair and moves toward the camera. After a moment the video ends. Jack felt utter contempt for Halloran like he had for no other person. He clicks on the next video and it's Halloran again sitting in the opposite chair. This time he was facing to the right. He had been drinking, and it was obvious:

Halloran: You know Joe, every once in a while, I ask, "God? Are you there?" And you know what I hear? Nothing. I don't even know if there is a God. We spend all this time selling religion and what do we get for it? Nothing. Empty pockets. No, actually we do get something. Something better. We get power. Power over people's will. We have politicians, police, celebrities power people from every walk of life and we can control by convincing them if they don't do what we say, they are going to Hell. Hell is the greatest sales tool ever created. When I was a kid, my mother always made us dress up for church. She had just become Catholic because they helped us financially. You see we were dirt poor in a wealthy town. My mother was obsessed with status. My father left her for some tart showgirl in New York City. I think I saw all of five times growing up. I think he hated my mother so much, he couldn't stand to be near her. I actually didn't blame him. She was detestable. She was the biggest phony I have ever seen and I hated her for that. She played the innocent grieving widow for so long. I didn't even know we were poor until I was in high school. She manipulated people so expertly that I started doing the same without even realizing. I also hated her for the beatings. She would beat us just for entertain-ment. But everything changed for me when I was fourteen. My mother wanted to go on some retreat in Colorado so she sent me to my great Aunt's house in Dallas, no Sunnyvale. 363 Michael Lane. I guess that's outside of Dallas. My great Aunt Gert was so old that she never got off the couch. She had just about every meal delivered and all I had to do was spend about an hour a day with her. It was supposed to be only for a weekend but my mother didn't come back for me for two and half months. It was summer and Gert's house was sweltering during the day so I left. Fortunately, Gert had a car so I took it and wandered around the area. After a while I would take some money from her. She thought I was going to the movies and sometimes I did. But one night I was at the house and I couldn't sleep. Gert was passed out on the couch as usual so I changed the channel and I found this preacher- Tilton, Robert Tilton was his name. He was in a suit and had this tall hair and he was on fire! This guy was preaching, crying, yelling and selling! He was doing this slick infomercial and he was selling books and trinkets and stupid stuff. I started asking around about this guy and you know that he would preach fire and brimstone and then do you know what he did? He told people that God would heal their sicknesses, fix their cars and 'supernaturally' pay their bills, if they would send him what he called a '$1000 faith promise'. This was brilliant! He literally got suckers to send him a grand! He was making a fortune! Once I saw how easy it was to get money and power with religion I was hooked.

McHenry (off camera): Why did you leave Texas?

Halloran: My mother. When she was done with her Colorado Sisters of the Perpetual Baloney retreat, she came and got me. Oh, and by the way, she got married while she was there. That selfish bitch didn't even ask me or call me or anything! Sprung it right on me at Gert's house. I thought the guy was the taxi driver. Dick Sermanelli. His name suited him, all right. First, he thought he'd try and be my friend. He bought me stuff and for a while that's all he was good for. Then, he wanted more kids. My mother was 41 years old and this asshat wanted to start another family! So, I have three half siblings with this guy. The funny thing is that my mother told him my father had died in Vietnam. Every- body thought my father was dead, because good Catholics don't ever get divorced. Those two nitwits believed that right up until the car ac- cident that killed my mother. I was a junior in high school. Dick had survived and the kids were at home with me. They were on their way to do layman's marriage counseling on a winter night. Once ol' Dick got out of the hospital, he had no need for me anymore. He decided to go back to Colorado and take 'his' kids with him. I thought I was go- ing, too. I even got early acceptance to a few colleges in the Denver area.

McHenry: Didn't you go to college in Long Island?

Halloran: Yup, Bradentown.

McHenry: What happened?

Halloran: Dick left me there. About two weeks before I was supposed graduate from high school, Dick piles us in all in the car. It was a Friday night. There's tons of luggage and other stuff in the car. Dick says we were going on a trip upstate. My siblings didn't look happy but I believed him. He says we need to make a stop at the rectory to speak with Father Somebody. Dick pulls up to the rectory and tells me to wait. He goes in for about two minutes. He comes back out and tells me the Father Whatshisname wants to talk to me about college or something. I went in thinking he just wanted to give me a pep talk. I had to pee anyway so I go in and the priest says to me, 'Welcome. We're glad to have you here.' I didn't understand at first. I didn't have any luggage and I didn't really know this guy. I forgot about the toilet as I heard the car pull away fast. THE BASTARD DUMPED ME OFF LIKE A FRIGGIN ORPHAN! Can you believe that? I wasn't even eighteen yet! The lousy SOB left me without a single word! (Sobbing lightly) We didn't even argue. We got along. We weren't close but we were civil.

McHenry: Geez, that's terrible.

Halloran: It wasn't a total loss. I was able to keep a little money my mother left me. Dick signed over guardianship of me to Father Guy-whatever for the few months that I had left as a minor. Then I was an adult and had to do everything myself. Saint Anthony's Seminary took me as a late entry and I started school in January.

McHenry: After everything that happened, you still wanted to become a priest?

Halloran: Yep. I even thought I would actually try to help people. But you what I learned even before leaving seminary? People are monsters. My mother, my father, Dick, laymen, nuns, even children. They are all monsters and by becoming a priest I could put myself above them. If I couldn't help them, I would control them.

McHenry: I became a priest because I just didn't want to work too hard. I thought with all the money the church takes in, I'd have it easy. I just had to work a couple of days a week and the church would take care of me.

Halloran: Joe, it's like I told you. No one is going to take care of you. People don't go to church anymore. Only old people and immigrants. We have to keep forcing them to come. If you get a good area, like Boston, a good chunk of New York and New Jersey, Connecticut, there's a high number of Catholics in the area. We gotta keep selling them hellfire. Keep them coming in and keep them scared. That gives us the power, but it doesn't keep the money rolling in like it used to. This whole thing with the girls started off as a side business. But, damn! I never thought it would bring the kind of cash we've scene. I told Shackelton that once I get to 5 million, I am moving to Florida and retire. Fortunately, the Archdiocese has so many cases of abuse, they'll never catch us. Those idiots who can't control themselves with the altar boys never learned to cover their tracks. Friggin perverts.

Jack couldn't watch anymore. It was 12:30am. He copied everything to disk and the to the cloud. He called Stanton, knowing it was late. "Hello, Stanton? It's Jack Chase."

Stanton was sleeping. "Hey Jack. What have you?"

"I have it all. Halloran, McHenry and even video of them talking about the operation and mentioning Shackelton. Connections to Atwell. It's everything."

"You uploaded to the cloud?"

"Yeah, Just now."

"Awesome. Keep your cover for now after we reviewed the files. See if you can get some girls to talk."

"Will do. We still on for tomorrow morning?"

"Yeah, 11am. Drive to Westford and text me."

"Right. See you then."

Jack shut everything down. He put copies of the files on an external drive then locked it in his floor safe. As he got ready for bed, he realized he needed an excuse for running out of the mixer and taking Martha Benson with him. Jack decided to tell him that Martha took sick and be brought her home. He lay on his bed and did his best to set aside all the pictures and video he watched. He was determined to stop Halloran and Shackelton whatever the cost.

It was a warm sunny spring day as Jack pulled onto Route 2 east. He enjoyed the drive and thought he'd take the back roads home after meeting Stanton. He took I-495 north for a few miles to the Boston Rd. exit. He pulled off at a convenience store and called Stanton. "I'm at the Cumby's just off the highway."

"All right, Jack. Come meet me at the Benton's across in the shopping area down the street."

"Will do."

Jack pulled out onto Route 110 and caught the green light at the intersection. He drove another 50 yards and pulled into the plaza. He parked and started to walk up to the building. Stanton was just inside the vestibule when a black sedan drove up an several shots peppered the entryway into the restaurant. Several people were grazed but Stanton was gravely wounded. Jack ran up the door and saw Stanton on the floor. "Stanton! Are you all right?"

"I'm hit!"

Jack saw that he was losing a lot of blood. "Chase! Listen to me! Someone talked, someone found out we were trying to get Halloran!"

"Who? Stay with me, Stanton!"

"I don't know. But it's someone who will lose if we get Halloran."

"Did Shackelton get out?"

"No, he's still being held at Devens."

"Someone at the bureau?"

"Not sure. Remember Halloran has powerful friends. Keep a watch out. Trust no one. Don't let them find you out."

Stanton passed out and Jack held him until the ambulance came. It was a little unnerving to have someone shot in front of you, even for a seasoned investigator. Jack knew he had to find the leak. He stuck around and waited for the police to come.

Jack drove back home. Alma was fixing lunch. "You're home late."

"We have a mole."

"Are you kidding?"

"No. They got to Stanton."

"What happened?"

"Drive by shooting. They knew where he was going to be and when. It has to be someone in the bureau."

"What are you going to do?"

"I don't think they know who I am. I think I will find a hotel somewhere no one really knows me and try to figure out what's going on."

"How long will you be gone?"

"I'd like to button this up this week. Someone's on to us, it's only a matter of time until they figure out who I am."

"This is getting dangerous, Jack. I don't want you to get hurt."

"I know, Sweetie. But I have to see this through. Those girls are depending on me."

"All right. Just be careful, please."

Jack spent the rest of the day with Alma and then found a hotel for Monday night.

The next morning, Jack was apprehensive as he threw his bag in the car. Alma was worried as well. "Are you sure they don't know who you are?"

"I'm pretty sure."

"That's not very reassuring."

"I know. I won't know until I can establish contact with the FBI. Stanton's not only down physically, his cover has been blown. I haven't spoken with him much since I went undercover, so it's not on my end."

"Just be careful. I know you can't call me but try to wrap this up quick, please."

Alma hugged Jack. "I will, I promise."

Jack pulled into the school parking lot and knew he had to be convincing. He thought a preemptive strike would be the best defense. He entered through the front door, checked in with Moira and asked if Father Halloran had come in yet. "No, Father Stevens. I have not heard from him yet."

"Thanks, Moira. I will head down to his office and wait for him." Jack smiled but left quickly. He knew he had first period free but he knew he had to get to Halloran before Chapel. Jack met Halloran as he came up to his office door. "Father Halloran! Do you have a moment?"

"Yes, of course."

"I wanted to explain about the mixer. After you left her, Martha came out of the room throwing up. I tended to her and decided to bring her home. I hope you didn't mind. I would have called you but I don't have your cell number."

"Ah, that explains it. Not to worry, Father Stevens, you did the right thing. I fear that most of Martha's issues are emotional so it stands to reason it would affect her that way."

"Good, I'm glad we cleared that up. I was concerned that I overstepped my authority."

"Oh, no. The health and welfare of our students is top priority. Think nothing of it."

"All right, thanks."

"See you in chapel."

Halloran smiled and stepped into his office. Jack made his was towards the Chapel. He entered the sanctuary and sat down. He was alone so he pulled out his cell phone and tapped on the app that was connected to the hidden cameras in Halloran's office. He saw that he was on the phone. Jack turned up the sound enough to eavesdrop on the phone call:

Halloran: What do you mean they tried to kill him? He is a fed! Are they nuts?

Unheard response.

Halloran: You're not serious? Then who was it?

Unheard response.

Halloran: I don't believe it. If that's true then we need to get out of town and very far away.

Unheard response.

Halloran: Look I have a friend at the Archdiocese but,

Unheard response.

Halloran: All right. Let's hope that it was the Mafia. I only have limited contact with them as customers, they are not involved in the operation.

Unheard response.

Halloran: We all need to start praying. If the Knights are involved, we're through!

Jack heard a noise and looked up. Father McHenry had just come up to the lectern. Jack stuffed his phone into his pocket and looked up at McHenry. "Angry Birds. Can't get enough."

"I'm a Candy Crush man, myself. Dang things."

The two men smiled, even though Jack knew there was a devil behind the collar. He continued the act as the chapel filled up with students. Father Halloran came in as the last few students filled in the back. He smiled at the other priests as he took to the podium. Halloran pontificated for a while but he seemed calmer than the first time. He again spoke on the evils of the flesh and then finished. He nodded at the rest of the priests and headed out as quickly as he arrived. Jack noticed an uneasiness with him and figured it was related to the earlier phone call. Jack left the chapel and went to the teacher's lounge for a coffee. He saw Father Blake and Sister Rose sitting at a table. He thought he would see what Sister Rose knew, since Halloran mentioned her as a co-conspirator. "Blessings, all. How are you doing?"

Father Blake responded. "We are well."

"I noticed Martha Benson wasn't in school today."

"Yes. Father Halloran suspended her. There is a hearing next week on whether or not she'll be allowed back or expelled."

"We're in the business of forgiveness, aren't we? I hope she is able to come back."

As Father Blake got up, he sneered, "You'd think," and walked out of the lounge. "Sister Rose. How are you?"

"Fine." She didn't seem like talking. "You know, I heard Father Halloran mention you earlier. Something about your 'retirement plan'?"

All the color dropped from her face. Jack continued. "Since I'm new here and my last parish didn't have a very good plan, I was wondering if you could tell me about your plan? I may want to convert it over."

"Excuse me." Sister Rose got very nervous and rushed out of the room. Jack had succeeded in rattling her and since he had another free period, he tuned into Halloran's office. He went to the bathroom and used an earpiece. Halloran was sitting at his desk with a glass and a bottle of scotch, rubbing his head. After about five minutes, the was a frantic knock at the door. "I'm busy! Come back later!"

"I need to talk to you! Let me in!"

Halloran got up and opened the door. Sister Rose pushed her way in. She saw the half glass of booze and downed it. Halloran was highly annoyed. "What the hell is the matter?"

"That new teacher! He knows something! Something about what we did!"

"Calm down, Rose. He can't know anything."

"He asked me about my retirement plan. He said he wanted to convert his old one to ours!"

"Look, he hasn't been here a full week. He couldn't have suspected anything remotely close."

"Still, he gave me the creeps. I want out. Now."

"You can't. You have to know that the Knights are involved."

"Knights? You mean the Knights of Saint Mary?"

"Yes. We must tread lightly. They have members all through society and if they find out what we've been doing, we are ruined."

"We're more than ruined! They'll hunt us down!"

"I am trying to work on a plan. If we do one more delivery, we can take the money we have and leave. We'll go somewhere they can't find us."

"You'll have to leave the priesthood. I will have to leave the sister-hood."

"It'll be for the best. We can get new identities and start over."

"All right."

"Just keep doing your job and in three days it'll all be over."

Jack was intrigued. He was about to look up the Knights of Saint Mary when he got a text. It was Agent Tasker. It was a coded message to meet after school. He responded in kind and went to class.

After school, Jack climbed into his car and drove to the rendezvous spot to meet Tasker. It was the Sartucci's restaurant inside Alewife Station in Cambridge. Jack stopped at a McDonald's restaurant to change out of his vestments so as not bring attention to himself. He waited until Tasker had entered the building. He put on a ball cap and a windbreaker with a high collar. Once he was sure the coast was clear, he went into the restaurant. Tasker was in the back of the restaurant. "We need to make this quick."

"Go."

"Good news and bad news. Good news is that Stanton will survive. He's critical but stable. The surgeries went well. None of the shots hit any vital organs."

"That's good. Give him my best. The bad news?"

"The leak came from within the Agency."

"Tell me something I don't know."

"Have you ever heard of Catholic Fraternal Orders?"

"Yeah like the Knights of Columbus?"

"Yes. There is one that is not very well known but has been operating for centuries."

"Let me guess. The Knights of St. Mary."

Tasker was surprised. "You are every bit the investigator. Yes, the Knights of St. Mary are a very old and very specific order. You could call them the Catholic FBI. They have been known to have members in every part of society."

"Makes sense, but why did they go after Stanton?"

"They weren't after Stanton, they're after Halloran. They thought that Stanton was meeting was him and well you know the rest."

"Sloppy."

"Come again?"

"If they were after me, thinking I was Halloran, then their intel is off. That means they have someone on the inside of the FBI."

"We believe they hacked Stanton's computer. That's why they may have thought you were Halloran. Maybe they thought Halloran was trying to cut a deal."

"Like I said, sloppy. If they have that kind power to get intel, they should have known that Stanton wasn't meeting Halloran."

"True. So, what do you think happened?"

"If these Knights are as good as they say they are then there has to be something else, something they know or are searching for."

"Right. I will keep searching. Meanwhile, do you have Halloran's files?"

Jack reached into his pocket and pulled out a thumb drive. "Here. When do you think I can pull out?"

"Soon. The thing is that we'll need to recover the original files but we'll have to get a court order to search his office. One last thing."

"What's that?"

"Shackelton's escaped from prison."

"How?"

"He had help. We think it's the last few members of his old gang. He was smuggled out through the laundry. The laundry service had reported the van stolen but the word didn't get to Devens before he got away."

"Perfect. Any other good news?"

"No but a warning. Not only does Shackelton know who you are, there is a better than average chance that he'll try to contact Halloran. He could easily blow your cover. Be careful."

"Thanks for the heads up."

Jack waited until Tasker left. He went to the bathroom for five minutes and left the restaurant. Rush hour traffic was tapering off so he pulled out onto Route 2 and headed west. He made reservations on Hanscom Air Force base at the Airman Hotel. He figured he'd be safe there and it was close enough to the school. He called Alma. "Hey Babe."

"Hey. How are things?"

"They've been better. I need you to take a trip."

"Where?"

"Go up to Maine. The Berwicks. Find a small, comfortable off the beaten track kind of place."

"Okay but why?"

"Shackelton's escaped from prison. I'm sure I'm on his short list."

"Oh, my. Do you think he'd come after you?"

"Yes, and I wouldn't put it past him to use you as leverage."

"Wow. What about Courtney?"

"She's in upstate New York visiting friends. I doubt he can get to her."

"Okay. I will leave ASAP."

"Thanks, Hun. I love you."

"I love you, too"

Jack slept a little better knowing his loved ones were out of harm's way. It's was safe to assume that Shackelton would try to contact Halloran. The problem was how to make sure Shackelton didn't blow his cover before Jack had a chance to nail Halloran and the other involved. He knew the files would not only tie Halloran to Shackelton's trafficking operation but it would also prove that Halloran had Mary Atwell elim- inated. Jack remembered Janice Marston. He only had the theory that

Halloran, or his accomplices, killed Marston by mistake, thinking she was Atwell. Jack got an idea. He knew the only thing Halloran was really afraid of were the Knights of Saint Mary. He sent off an email to Tasker and she responded, 'proceed with extreme caution'. Jack was confident he could pull it off.

Jack entered the school and greeted Moira as he checked his mailbox. There was nothing of consequence so he proceeded to chapel. Halloran was more subdued today and left in a hurry once he dismissed the students to first period. It was Tuesday, so there was no confessional. Jack waited about 20 minutes and then went to Halloran's office. "Good morning, Father."

"Good Morning." Halloran was anxious. He was waiting for something, or someone.

"I've been meaning to discuss something with you."

"Really? What is it?" Halloran was faking any interest.

"We haven't really gotten to know each other. I figured it would take some time so I like us to meet on a regular basis."

"All right. When is good with you?"

"I have first period free four days a week. How about Tuesdays after chapel?"

"Fine. We'll do that but unfortunately today I have an appointment and they're supposed to call first."

"Oh? We Knights of Saint Mary prefer to drop in. It's less formal."

Halloran became extremely pale. Then he became even more nervous. "You're from the Knights?"

"Let's just say I'm here to help."

"They sent you to deal with me?"

Jack ignored the question. "Father Halloran, I'd like you to humor me for a moment. Why do you think we're here?"

"Well, obviously there's been some misunderstanding."

"Enlighten me, please."

"The rumors about my disciplining the students. I am only doing what I think is best for them."

"Like, showing them what not to do, I assume."

"Yes! They are like cauldrons of hormones and without the proper guidance may end up in grave trouble."

"How do you deliver this guidance, Father?"

"Well, I counsel them and talk to them."

"Is that all?"

"Of course! What are you implying?"

"We've been tracking you for quite some time. The Archdiocese has been very generous in accommodating you but now, since the disappearance of Sister Mary Atwell, we cannot condone your 'style' of discipline any longer."

Halloran swallowed hard and sat down at his desk. "What will happen to me?"

"That isn't up to me. My job is to alert you and set up a meeting with the Council. It would help to turn over all files and media to me now. Cooperate and things may turn out better."

"If I turn everything over, will the spare my life?"

"It's likely."

Halloran opened the door that went into the closet and brought out the chest. "This is everything I have."

"What about your computer? Is there anything on that?"

"No, I download everything I record to external media."

"All right. You will do everything you normally do except meet with students alone."

"Yes, I will."

Jack stood up as he was leaving. "Oh, one more thing. Do you know where we could find Mr. Shackelton?"

"Dear Lord, you know about Shackelton!"

"Yes, it seems he left prison earlier than he should have."

"He escaped?"

Jack nodded. "Do you know where he is?"

"No, I don't. You must believe me!"

"If he should contact you, you are to let me know immediately. Do not tell him that I've made contact with you and make him think everything is normal."

"I will."

Jack was pretty pleased with himself. He went to class and the rest of the morning was uneventful. He had just finished lunch when Father Halloran came into the teacher's lounge. "Father Stevens, a word?"

Jack wiped his mouth and went outside the door of the lounge with Halloran. "I just spoke with Shackelton. He is expected me to give him a list of girls. We call it the 'college list'."

"I figured as much. Where are you meeting him?"

"At the rectory. At six tonight."

"All right. Make sure none of the girls are there. Also bring Sister Rosa. They'll want to talk to her."

"Right. Six o'clock."

Jack finished his last class of the day. He didn't have a last period so he left early and drove to Alewife. He dialed Tasker's number. "Halloran set up a meeting with Shackelton, tonight at six."

Tasker was notably surprised. "You found him?"

"Didn't have to-he called Halloran."

"Where's the meeting?"

"At the Rectory. 35 Chestnut St."

"Okay, I'll have a team of agents there."

"See you then."

As Jack was leaving Alewife, a beige sedan pulled out and appeared to be following him. He seemed to recognize the car but then it turned off. He shook it off and continued to Hanscom. When he got to his hotel, he opened the trunk and took out a small metal box. Jack went to his room and looked around as he entered. He changed to street clothes and ordered pizza. After he ate, Jack put the metal box on the table. He pressed a button on the box under the handle and a biometric pad next to it lit up. He drew his finger across the pad and the box clicked open. Inside was a holstered 9mm Glock and a box of ammo. Jack pulled the pistol from the holster and cleared the chamber and checked the clip. Fully loaded. He took another clip from his suitcase and loaded it. He put on the holster with the pistol and stuffed the clip in an inside pocket in his jacket. It was 5:20 so he decided to leave.

Jack pulled onto Route 128 south and drove towards the Route 2 exit. Traffic was light since he was headed towards Boston. He passed back by Alewife and stopped at a light. He drove to the rotary near Fresh Pond and he noticed the same beige sedan from before. He decided to see if it was following him so he took the Concord Ave exit and drove up through Belmont. The sedan followed so he doubled back through Belmont to Route 2 east. The sedan continued to follow him. It was 5:50 and Jack needed to get to the rectory. He gunned the motor and cut off a semi, successfully losing the sedan. Jack drove faster to get some distance. Once he was satisfied that he lost the sedan, he headed straight for the rectory.

Jack arrived at the rectory on time. He saw Halloran and McHenry in a car parked at the front door. "Good evening, Gentlemen. Is Sister Rosa here?"

Halloran gulped hard. "No, I haven't seen her."

"We will deal with her later. Shall we?"

The two men were nervous as they entered the building. Jack stayed behind them. He noticed that there was a cleaning crew unloading equipment on the side of the building. Inside the large parlor were three men, one in a suit. The man in the suit had his back to them. Halloran and McHenry entered the parlor and the floor squeaked. The man in the suit reacted and turned around. It was Shackelton. Jack put on sunglasses in the foyer stood near the door. Shackelton was friendly and polite. "Good evening, Gentlemen. You have my shipment ready?"

Halloran was less than confident. "Yes. We do."

"All right. Let's finish up." Shackelton gestured to one of his henchmen and they went to a closet. He reached in and pulled out a briefcase. Shackelton took the briefcase from him and opened it. It was full of cash. Halloran took the case and fidgeted. "What's the matter, Father? You don't look so well."

"No problem, I've just been overworked. A little tired, that's all."

"Oh, I see. You didn't come and see me in jail this time. I waited a long time."

"School was starting and I was making sure the next shipment was in order."

"Oh, that explains it. So, let get them." Shackelton was emotionless.

"All right." Halloran started to sweat even more. McHenry was pale and clammy. Jack ducked into side room so Shackelton wouldn't see him. As the three men came out of the front door, SWAT teams and agent swarmed in from nowhere. Jack looked outside and was relieved that Tasker was on time. The two henchmen reached for their guns and Jack has his pistol out. Tasker whipped out her pistol and pointed it at the men. "Don't do it. Get your hands up."

Tasker came up along with several of the cleaning crew and arrested the five men. Halloran turned to look at Jack. "I thought you were with the Knights?"

"I could be, couldn't I?"

Halloran had a confused look on his face as an FBI agent approached the men.

Shackelton, turned and looked at Jack. "Chase? You're in on this?" Shackelton reached for Jack and grabbed him by the shirt. Both men went down but Shackelton got up and ran back into the rectory. Jack got up and ran in after him. Shackelton pulled over various small statues and vases to try to slow Jack down. He ducked into a vestibule and let Jack run by him. He moved too soon and Jack heard him. Jack turned around and caught up with him at the top of the grand staircase. Shackelton went for Jack's throat. "I should have killed you in the woods!"

"You're going down, Shackelton! Permanently!" The two men struggled until Jack delivered a sharp blow to the abdomen, dropping Shackelton to his knees. He made a surprise move to throw Jack down the stairs, but Jack countered it. Jack ended up riding Shackelton down the stairs, and hitting him on the way down. Jack got up first and grabbed Shackelton. Shackelton tried to throw a final punch but Jack reached back and laid him out on the floor. Jack picked him up twisted his arm behind his back. Shackleton popped his head back and butted Jack, stunning him for a moment. Shackelton threw a punch and knocked Jack back again. He threw another punch and Jack blocked it. Jack threw a standard 1-2 boxing combo and Shackelton went down hard. Jack rolled him over and held him.

"That's enough!" Tasker came in with her pistol drawn.

Shackelton was red faced. "You'll pay for this Chase! I swear it!"

Jack just smiled and rubbed his hand. Another agent handcuffed Shackelton and escorted him out. "You enjoyed that, didn't you?" Agent Tasker moved closer to Jack.

"You better believe it."

"We'll still need to get a court order for those files."

"Don't bother. Halloran gave them to me."

"How in the world do you get him to do that?"

Jack smiled. "Opportunity."

Jack spent another night on Hanscom. He got dressed in street clothes and drove over to St. Baskins for the final time. He walked into the office and Moira was sitting at her desk. "Hello Moira."

"Father Stevens! You aren't wearing your collar!"

"Yes, well actually my name is Jack Chase and I've been working for the FBI."

"You what? FBI? You mean you aren't actually a teacher?"

"It's a long story. The reason I came back was to explain what has happened to the faculty and staff." Jack hands her a sealed brown envelope. "All the documentation and authorizations are here. "Father Halloran and Father McHenry have been arrested.

"What on earth for?"

"It's pretty bad. The Archdiocese is sending a representative to explain what happened to the students and provide counseling. If you could call the staff together in the lounge, I can give them the Reader's Digest version."

Moira was still in some shock but she made the announcement that Chapel was canceled and that all the students should remain in homeroom until further notice. She then assembled the faculty and staff in the teacher's lounge. Jack stood silent for a while once everyone had come in. He noticed Sister Rosa was missing. Sister Agnes, the physical education teacher spoke first. "What's this all about?"

Jack stood up behind Moira as she addressed the room. "Thank you for coming in on such short notice. We have a grave situation that has resulted in the arrest of Fathers Halloran and McHenry."

There was a collective gasp and the room became eerily quiet. "Most of you know this man as Father Stevens, the new English teacher that replaced Father Malone."

"Thanks, Moira. I'll take it from here. As Moira said, most of you know me as Father Stevens. My real name is Jack Chase and I am a special agent with the FBI. For the last three years, several of the graduating seniors and a few juniors from St. Baskins have disappeared. Many of you thought they went to college or lost track of them after they graduated. Some of you also may remember a young teacher that used to work here, Sister Mary Atwell. We have proof that several graduates were abducted and sold into the sex trade overseas. We also have proof that Halloran and McHenry assisted in supplying a human trafficking ring with girls from this school. I was sent here to investigate and prevent anymore girls from being taken."

Sister Theresa from the Math Department raised her hand. "Were they the only ones involved?"

"No. We have proof of others here involved in helping Father Halloran in grooming the girls for sale. He took advantage of them under the guise of 'discipline' and he shot video to show his buyer."

There was murmurs of shock and disgust from most of the room. Father Blake spoke. "Did Halloran name the others involved?"

"We are withholding the names until the people can be properly charged. If anyone here has information concerning this matter, it would be in your best interest to come forward. Now the Archdiocese is going to offer additional counseling to any one that wants it. They are also working with us to recover the victims and reunite them with their families. Are there any other questions?" No one dared raise their hands. Any comment may suggest that they had some involvement in the crime. "That's all I have. If you want to contact the FBI about this, I have the number of the agent in charge. Thank you."

Jack stayed for a few minutes as the faculty filed out of the room. Moira was visibly upset. Jack felt bad for her. "I'm so sorry, Moira."

"I am too. But something concerns me."

"What is it?"

"Sister Rosa didn't show up this morning. She has always been prompt. I remember only one time she called out sick."

Jack got into his car. It was just before ten. He was going to miss the students but he already missed his own. He was still bothered by Sister Rose's disappearance. Jack brought up Tasker's number on his phone. He had it connected by Bluetooth to the car so he called her as he started to drive home. "Can you do me a favor?"

"Sure."

"Can you check to see if Sister Rose Antonetti was arrested last night?"

"Hold on." Jack could hear papers rustling. "No, we have a warrant out for her arrest but we haven't found her yet."

"Let me know when you do, please. Just tying up loose ends."

"I can do that."

"Thanks."

Jack breathed easier as he turned onto Route 2 west. He still had a couple of days of leave so he was thinking of meeting Alma in the Berwicks. He was already packed so he started to dial Alma when he noticed that same beige sedan behind him. Jack wasn't sure if the sedan was following him so he held off calling Alma. He drove in silence until he got to Route 128 north. The Lexington Service Area was just half a mile up from the exit, so once he got onto 128, he stayed in the slow lane until he pulled into the plaza. The sedan followed and park two rows behind him. Jack locked his car and felt for his gun. He got out of the car and locked it as he went into the building. He saw a man dressed in black get out of the sedan and head toward the building. Jack crossed the dining area and lingered at a sunglasses kiosk until the man came in. He went into the bathroom. The man in black followed him. The man checked the urinals and then started looking in the stalls. As he stood at the last row of toilets, Jack pushed him hard into an empty stall. The stunned man turned around and Jack had his gun to the man's forehead. "Who are you and why are you following me?"

"Father Stevens, I mean you no harm."

"Who are you? How do you know my name?"

The man reached into his coat. "Easy there, Johnny Cash."

"My identification." Jack reached in and took the wallet. It had a silver ornate crest in it, about the size of a police badge. The man had a slight foreign accent. "I am a Knight of the Holy Order of St. Mary."

"Really? Why are you following me?"

"You are a teacher at St. Baskins, yes?"

"No. I am an investigator."

"You are not Father Philip Stevens?"

"That was my cover. My real name is Jack Chase."

"Then our information is flawed."

"I should say so. You guys shot a friend of mine."

"Yes. It was a grave error. It was thought that Halloran was meeting a prospective client for his 'services'."

"Fortunately, the FBI agent survived."

"The Knights are not as well informed as we used to be. We will take care of Mr. Stanton's hospital bills and anything else he may need."

"How did you know about the meeting?" Jack put his gun away as the men left the bathroom.

"We have members throughout the country and in the government. We had suspected Halloran's wrongdoing for several years. Unfortunately, we did not have enough proof to arrest him."

"Arrest him? I don't think you have any jurisdiction here. You had better leave it to the FBI. They'll take care of him."

"The Knights are connected in a way that regular law enforcement is not."

"I'm not sure that's a good thing."

"Nevertheless, we will handle this internally."

"Listen, Mr.?"

"Antonio."

"Mr. Antonio.

"I caution you to not interfere with a federal investigation."

"The Vatican has very specific rules regarding this type of thing. Father Halloran and his co-conspirators will be extradited and face the Sacred Court."

"I think the FBI will have something to say about that."

"Maybe."

"Look let's say that you guys end up with Halloran. What about the girls he's sold into slavery?"

"We have returned the ones we have found. About 75%. We have a team working on finding the rest. Don't worry."

"There is one thing you don't have."

"And what is that?"

"Proof. The FBI has Halloran's files. They won't just turn them over to a shadowy Catholic organization."

"They probably won't need to do that."

Jack was leery of Antonio's next words. "Why?"

"Let's just say we have someone who will give testimony against Halloran."

"There's only one other-", Jack stopped mid-sentence. Antonio smiled. "You are a good detective, Mr. Chase."

"Sister Rosa wasn't at the meeting this morning."

"She will live a simple, life. Probably very solitary, but at least she will live."

"You know I will have to report this."

"I would expect nothing less. Good Day, Mr. Chase."

Jack was still pondered the clandestine reach of the Knights of Saint Mary. He sat down in a booth and called Tasker. "You aren't going to believe this."

"Let me guess. You know who posted bail for Halloran?"

"Wow, that was fast. And, yes, I believe I do."

Jack and Alma pulled into the driveway just before four O'clock. Jack was glad he and Alma spent the last four days in Maine. It was a nice, restful time and Jack felt refreshed. He brought in the luggage and decided he'd unwind before unpacking. He joined Alma on the couch as she was watching tv. "Jack did you see this?" He looked at the screen and it was a breaking news story:

"Breaking News. A local human trafficking ring was shut down by the FBI. The ring was operating out of the St. Baskins Preparatory School in Watertown. Three members of the school's faculty were implicated in the ring, Father A. Joseph Halloran, Sister Rose Antonetti, and Father Neil McHenry. The investigation has extensive evidence that the three suspects not only sold graduating students into slavery, but sexually abused them during school hours. The FBI is not releasing the names of the students nor the agents that were involved in the investigation."

Alma cuddled next to Jack. "I'm so glad this thing is over."

"Me too. I had to do quite an acting job with these guys." Jack shifted to nuzzle her neck.

Alma thought for a moment. "You know Jack, it's quite a black eye on the Catholic church. I didn't grow up Catholic but I had a lot of friends who did. The local parish was full of really great people."

Jack nodded. "It's true with any social organization. The Boy Scouts, the YMCA, they are all great institutions, but they don't establish the moral code that folks need; they just enhance it."

"You mean it's not their job."

"Right. It starts in the home. So many young people would turn out differently if they had fathers in the home. Our society is systematically removing the fathers from the home and it's wrecking these young kids. No respect for authority, no guidance, and they expect the schools to do it for them! And that's not even the underprivileged kids!"

"I guess what I'm saying is people like Halloran make it hard for the others who are trying to do the right thing."

"Sweetie, you're venting."

"I know. I just wish parents would do their job and that society would stop demonizing fathers."

"You are a good dad. Courtney is a wonderful young lady. Graduated college cum laude, accepted into several different Master's programs, you should be proud."

"I am. I'm so proud of her I could bust. She made us proud."

Shackelton was escorted through the prisoner entry gates at the Massachusetts Correctional Institute, Shirley, MA. His hands and feet were shackled to a chain around his waist. He was to remain there until his arraignment in three weeks. The agent that brought Shackelton in had the papers ready for the guard. "Shackelton, William. Age 45, height 6' 1", arraignment date, June 22."

"Thanks, we'll take it from here." The guard did not make eye contact.

The agent was holding the papers out. "Hey, I need a signature. The brass is pretty anal about these transfer orders."

"Okay." The guard scribbled on the papers and handed them back to the agent. "Here ya go." The guard took Shackelton and roughly pulled him through the gate. "Let's go, pervert." The agent thought it odd but assumed the guard had kids.

The guard continued to pull Shackelton into the prison, but took him away from the processing area. The guard brought him to an empty storage closet with a chair and said, "Wait here." The guard closed the door and locked it. Shackelton was trying to stand up and free himself when the door opened. Standing there were three men; the guard, another man dress in a black suit with a black shirt, and another man dressed in a sharp, black business suit. "My name is Antonio."

Shackelton was visibly scared. "Do I know you? I don't have any contacts in New York anymore."

"No Mr. Shackelton. You do not know me but I know you. I believe you know some of our associates, Father Halloran and Father McHenry."

"Who are you?"

"We are the protectors of the Catholic faith. And unfortunately, Mr. Shackelton, you are not in favor with our superiors."

Agent Tasker was sitting at her desk doing paperwork when a familiar voice entered the room. "Hey Partner."

"Stanton! Glad to see you back on your feet!"

"Nice to be back, even if it's desk duty."

"Oh, that won't last long. You'll drive us crazy enough to send you back out by the end of the week!"

"If for that long."

An agent comes into the room and grabs the tv remote. "Have you guys seen this?"

"The body of alleged human trafficker and former priest Neil McHenry was found floating in Fort Pond, Lancaster, only a few miles from the Massachusetts Correctional Institute, Shirley where he was being held until his arraignment. It was originally assumed that he had escaped, but now since he was only found a few miles from the facility he may have fallen victim to mob related activity. McHenry had been taken down during an undercover investigation by local Langston Vice Principal Jack Chase. Chase, a former Army Investigator, was hailed as a hero for the rescue of the Hanney Brothers and then again, a more recent rescue of his own students abducted by William Shackelton, an associate of McHenry. Chase was deputized by the FBI due to his extensive experience as an investigator. Mr. Chase has declined interviews-"

Jack clicked the tv off and pulled Alma over to him. "That's enough. I don't need my ego stroked that much."

Alma smiled as she rolled on her back so her head was on Jack's lap. "What do you want, Mr. Chase, Defender of the Innocent?"

"You, my dear."

"I thought you swore you'd get married first? You prude!"

"Yes. So, marry me."

"Wow, you are as romantic as a brick."

"I'm serious! Let's get married."

Alma sat up, very surprised. "Really? Are you sure?"

"Yes. We've both been married before, so there are no surprises. A simple ceremony. The weather is nice and we can do the reception here."

"Oh, Jack! Of course, I will marry you! But on one condition."

"What is it?"

"We do it in a month. I agree a small, simple ceremony is good, but I don't want a long engagement."

"A month it is then."

One week later, Jack was back at Langston High. He missed his kids. He was glad to be back home with his own faculty and staff. Jack thought about his experience at St. Baskins and made every effort to remind his students that they could come and talk to him anytime. Since the Lake Dennison incident, Jack wanted his kids to feel safe and protected. He was sitting in his office when Alma came in. "Hey there. Have you seen the news?"

"No, I'm afraid I'll be on it again."

"Very funny. You should see this."

Alma reached over him and clicked on a local news website. Jack turned up the sound:

Alleged child abuser and sex trafficker, A. Joseph Halloran a former priest at the St. Baskins Prep in Watertown, has disappeared from the St. Ignacious Parish in Cambridge where he was free on conditional bail. He was required to wear an ankle monitoring bracelet and prohibited from any contact with a minor. Halloran was scheduled to be arraigned on Tuesday federal court. If you have any information on the whereabouts of Halloran, call the FBI at this number.

Alma looked worried. "Do you think he is going to try to come after you?"

"No, I doubt it. I don't think he's that ambitious. Besides he's a coward. I'd be more concerned with Shackelton."

"Is he coming after you?"

"Only if he escapes again. He is pretty oily. If he hadn't done it before, he might have a better chance of doing it now. The FBI has him under 24-hour watch."

"I'm glad you feel that way. I'd be pretty nervous if he was still out there."

"No worries, hun. Besides my crimefighting days are done. I am now just a high school principal."

"Until someone threatens your kids again."

"I'll burn that bridge when I come to it." They both smile and continued their day.

Jack's day ended on a high note. Several of his top students were accepted into ivy league schools and he was thinking of planning some type of celebration. He walked up to his car as a small convertible pulled up to him. At the wheel was Mr. Antonio. "Mr. Chase! I am glad I caught you. I wanted to let you know that the situation with Halloran is settled."

"Should I ask how you settled it?"

"It would be prudent if you didn't."

"Then why bother to tell me?"

"The Knights of Saint Mary were impressed by your skills as an investigator. We would like you to consider joining us."

"I'm flattered but I'm neither catholic nor an investigator, anymore. I am a high school principal. This was a one-time thing."

"We realize that you may think us somewhat clandestine. I assure you that we have a just and honorable mission."

"Again thanks, but I am getting married in less than a month."

"Well, we certainly do not want to interfere with that, eh? I have been married for 22 years."

"And your wife approves of what you do for a living?"

"Of course! How do think I met her?"

"She is a Knight too?"

"We are a very diverse group, Mr. Chase."

"I'm beginning to see that."

"Besides that, I spend most of my time at my day job."

"And what would that be?"

Antonio smiled. "I'm an insurance broker in Shrewsbury."

Jack chuckled. "Nice to know you're local."

"Indeed, Mr. Chase. I must go but here is my card if you change your mind, or need insurance."

"Thanks."

Antonio climbs into the convertible. "And just so you know, not all of us are catholic."

Lightning Source UK Ltd.
Milton Keynes UK
UKHW010619071222
413495UK00001B/82